Shiloh

**Other westerns by
Dusty Rhodes**

Man Hunter

Jedidiah Boone

Treble Heart Books
1284 Overlook Dr.
Sierra Vista, AZ 85635-5512

The characters and events in this book are fictional, and any resemblance to persons, whether living or dead, is strictly coincidental.

ISBN: 1-931742-63-4

Visit the entire Treble Heart Books web
site including:
Treble Heart Books
MountainView Publishing (inspirational)
Sundowners (new Westerns imprint
November 2002)
http://www.trebleheartbooks.com

520-458-5602
Fax: 520-458-5618
Email: submissions@trebleheartbooks.com

Shiloh
by
Dusty Rhodes

SUNDOWNERS
The
Westerns division
of
Treble Heart Books

CHAPTER I

APRIL 8, 1865—Camp Douglas Prisoner of War Camp near Chicago, Illinois. Known as the "Death Camp."

The bleeding finally stopped. Shiloh winced and sucked a draft of air through clenched teeth. Searing pain knifed through him like a red-hot poker. He rolled his head and lifted it off the bare, slat-board bunk. His face screwed up into a grimace as he stared in horror at the gaping wound on his left forearm. White bone lay exposed through an opening two inches wide that started just below his elbow and angled down to near his wrist.

"That's a nasty cut," the old Confederate field doctor said, lowering his balding head to peer over the tiny spectacles that sat on the very tip of a bulbous nose. "I'm gonna have to sew that arm up."

Shiloh didn't answer. He resigned himself to what was about to happen and watched the doctor as he withdrew a long curved needle, a spool of black thread, and a half full bottle of whiskey from a worn black doctoring bag.

After threading the needle with a shaky hand, the doc doused Shiloh's cut with the golden liquid before tipping the bottle to his lips and taking a long swallow.

"I got nothing to give you, Son," Doc Williams told him. "This ain't gonna be easy but it's got to be done. I can spare a swig or two from my bottle if you like. It might dull the hurt some."

"Thanks anyway," Shiloh said. "Don't see how it could hurt much worse than it already does. Go on and get it over and done with."

Shiloh watched the old doctor stare at the wound over his glasses for a long minute before shaking his head and tightening the tourniquet another twist. Doc poured the open cut full of whiskey. White-hot fire shot up his arm in a paroxysm of pain.

Each stroke of the needle sent a stab of pain racing through him like a lightening bolt, jarring him to the very core of his being. To separate his mind from the hurt, Shiloh tried to think about something else.

He watched the doctor as he worked. The man seemed tired. It was no wonder. He worked night and day trying to keep the three hundred or so Confederate prisoners of war alive.

A thousand Confederate prisoners were interned in the camp before last winter. Three hundred eighty seven had been buried in shallow graves hacked from the frozen ground during the month of January alone. Without even a blanket, most had simply frozen to death.

The whole camp knew that the Union commander, Colonel Mattox, regularly stole money that was supposed to be used for food and blankets and medicine for the prisoners; it was an open secret.

The Union called this place Camp Douglas Prisoner of War Camp. The prisoners called it, 'The Death Camp'.

Shiloh laid his head back on his bunk and stared at the ceiling. He bit back the excruciating pain and swallowed screams that welled up in his throat each time the doctor pierced his skin with the shiny needle. As the old doc worked, he mumbled a steady stream of gibberish that Shiloh couldn't understand.

"If you're gonna talk, I wish you'd do it so a man could understand what you're saying," Shiloh mumbled through clenched teeth.

"I said, it's pure barbaric. Making two men fight each other like that. Like...like some kind of gladiators of something. When this war's over, you can bet your britches I'm gonna see the colonel's superiors hear about what went on in this place."

Shiloh eyed the doctor with an appreciative stare. He had heard it said the doc was from Arkansas somewhere around Fort Smith. Someone that had known him before the war said the doc gave up a successful practice to join up and fight for what he believed in. The man was barely beyond middle-aged, but looked much older. War did that to a man.

His thinning gray hair brushed straight back failed to hide balding spots. Deep turkey tracks lined bloodshot eyes in a reddish, puffy face. Heavy bags hung loose and flabby under the tiny spectacles and spoke of too many nights with too little sleep.

"You don't really think he's gonna let anybody walk out of here alive to tell anything do you?" Shiloh asked.

"You're lucky this fellow didn't kill you. Who was he? I never did hear his name."

"Jackson. His name was Tom Jackson. He was with the second infantry of Kentucky. He was just an overgrown kid trying to get home and desperate enough to try anything. I don't blame him none. Can't say I wouldn't do the same it they promised I could walk out free as a bird if I won."

"It's down right barbaric," the doc said, tying off the last stitch and pouring what was left from the bottle over the wound. "That bayonet could have opened up your belly instead of your arm. How many is it now?"

"Six," Shiloh replied sadly. "The worse part of it is, even if any of them had killed me, the Colonel wouldn't have let them walk out of here alive. That big sergeant of his would have shot 'em in the back before they got a mile down the road."

"How long you been in here, son?"

"I was captured in the fall of 'sixty-three. So let's see, this is early April. I guess it's going on a year and a half now. I plumb lost track. Like I say, it don't make no difference 'cause none of us will get out of here alive anyway."

"Why's the colonel so all fired set on seeing you dead? Never seen a man hate so hard."

"It all goes back to the battle of Shiloh in April of 'sixty-two. The Colonel had over a thousand Union soldiers under his command. They were dug in at a place called the 'Hornet's Nest.' They had beat back two Confederate charges before General Johnson ordered us to make an all out assault on the Union's position.

"I had just received a battlefield promotion to Captain of the First Cavalry. There wasn't much left of the company. It had a little over a hundred regulars and another fifty misfits from other outfits.

"I'll never know why they picked my company to spearhead the attack because the general himself was killed later that same day. It was a suicide mission from the start. None of us should have survived.

"My horse was shot out from under me before we got halfway up the hill. I managed to jump free and grab a rifle with a bayonet on it from a fallen soldier and led my men in a bayonet charge. I wasn't trying to be no hero or nothing, I just didn't know nothing else to do.

"I tell you, Doc, it was something to see, though. We went charging up that hill, as hard as we could run, right into a hail of bullets, screaming at the top of our lungs like a bunch of wild Indians. We must have put the fear of God in them or something. The colonel's blue bellies threw down their weapons and lit out. They left their cannons and everything. They just lit a shuck.

"I heard later the colonel was court-martialed for cowardice in the face of the enemy. It was only after I was captured and sent here, that I discovered he had been demoted and put in charge of this prisoner of war camp."

"So he blames you for his court-marshal and demotion," the doc said, leaning back in the straight chair and shaking his head.

"I reckon so."

"So that's why he has that sergeant of his, the one they call the 'Bear', set up these 'Battle of the Bayonets.' He wants to see you die by the same weapon you used to defeat him. Is that when you picked up the nickname Shiloh?"

"Yeah, my real name is Nathan Whittington. I reckon for some folks that's just too much to get out all in one breath, so everybody just took to calling me Shiloh."

"Well," the doc said, picking up his black bag and standing, "that's about all I can do for that arm right now. You best keep it still for awhile so you don't tear it open again. I'll look at it again in a day or two. It ain't gonna be much use to you for quite a spell. I'll see if I can scrounge up something to use for a sling. The less you move it around the quicker it's gonna heal."

"Thanks Doc, I'm obliged to you," Shiloh called out as he limped out the door on his gimpy leg.

Shiloh lay on his bunk, drew a long, shaky breath and stared at the ceiling, lost in his own swirling thoughts. When would all the killing stop? He had already seen enough in his twenty-two years to last him a lifetime.

After awhile he heard the supper bell ring. He'd skip supper, he decided. He couldn't bring himself to use what little energy he had left to walk the hundred yards or so to the mess hall. Besides, the slop they called food wasn't worth the effort.

He rolled to his side and felt his leg touch metal. Reaching his right hand, his fingers closed on the cold steel of a bayonet. It was Tom Jackson's bayonet, the man he had just killed.

Shiloh lifted it before his eyes, and slowly turned it. He stared at it for a long few minutes. Its edges were honed to razor sharpness. The point had been ground down until it was needle sharp.

The last rays of a setting sun filtered through the open door and skipped off the shiny metal, shooting streaks of light bouncing off the walls of the prisoners' barracks.

Traces of Shiloh's own blood still clung to the evil weapon. Another man had died. A good man. A man with dreams and hopes and plans for a future and maybe a ma and pa waiting back home for their son to return from war. Shiloh's heart hurt. A tear seeped from the corner of his pale green eyes and slowly traced a wet trail down his cheeks.

The sound of footsteps jerked his mind back to the present. He quickly sat upright and hurriedly slid a small wooden box from underneath his bunk. Lifting the lid, he added the bayonet to the five others inside.

"How come you weren't at supper?" Lester Posey asked as he tromped through the door. "Some of us was worried sick about you."

Lester was a long and lanky, sandy haired boy from Tennessee, just a few mountains over from Shiloh's own home. His ruddy complexion and peach fuzz whiskers gave him a boyish look though he was a year older than Shiloh. Lester had lost his left arm at the second battle of Bull Run, had been captured, and ended up in this hell hole. He was one of only a few fellow prisoners Shiloh could count as a friend. Most were afraid to have anything to do with him. They were afraid of incurring the wrath of the sergeant or of being selected as Shiloh's next opponent.

"Didn't figure it'd be worth the walk," Shiloh told his friend.

"It weren't," Lester said, flashing a grin that took up most of his face. "Boy, you shore whipped that old boy good today. Wish I could fight like that. I thought he had you a time or two, especially when he laid your arm open. You was bleeding like a stuck hog. How is it? Are you okay?"

"Yeah, I'm okay. The doc sewed it up. But I'd rather not talk about it if it's all the same to you."

"Good enough for him if you ask me. Good-bye and good riddance to bad rubbish. A man that would go against —"

"Lester," Shiloh interrupted harshly.

"Okay-okay, dag nab it. He just shouldn't of done it and he got what he had coming to him and that's all I'm gonna say about it."

The footsteps of several men approaching the barracks halted their conversation. Shiloh swung a glance at the door, expecting to see some of his fellow prisoners returning from supper.

Instead, the massive hulk of the sergeant of the guard filled the doorway, blocking out the last remnants of a dimming twilight from outside. He was a thick set giant of a man. Only slightly shorter than Shiloh's own six foot four inches but the sergeant would tip the scales at well over three hundred pounds.

His huge head seemed to cling deep-seated on his massive shoulders with no neck in between. Ham-size arms stretched the sleeves of the Union jacket that carried dirty sergeant stripes. Dark, beady eyes peered menacingly from under a heavily bearded face and fixed directly on Shiloh.

The big man shuffled into the barracks and headed toward Shiloh's bunk. As always, he was accompanied by a squad of heavily armed guards. When he spoke it sounded like an angry bullfrog croaking on a quiet summer night.

"You all healed up, Reb?" he asked, a cruel laugh spewing from his throat.

Shiloh didn't bother answering. Lester backed up against the plank wall, trying hard to make himself invisible.

"Stand up when I'm talking to you!" the man roared.

Shiloh rolled his head sideways and sliced his gaze to lock eyes with the giant. For a long minute they glared at each other, competing in a silent combat of wills, neither seemingly willing to be the first to look away.

Slowly, with no small difficulty, Shiloh swung his legs to the floor and pulled himself to his full height before slouching defiantly before the sergeant.

"I got some news for you," the big man growled. "You got another fight tomorrow. Thought you'd want to know since it'll be your last one. This one ain't gonna be no pushover like the others. He come in yesterday with the last bunch of prisoners. His name is Boone Le Feve. He's a Cajun from New Orleans. Supposed to be some kind of expert at knife fighting I hear tell."

"Shiloh's in no shape to fight again this quick," Lester spoke up, his voice quivering with fear. "Can't you see his arm is cut half off?"

"Looks fit to me," the sergeant bellowed, accompanied by an evil laugh. Turning on his heels he wobbled out the door, calling over his shoulder, "You sleep good now, Reb."

Morning came slow. Shiloh hadn't slept a wink all night; he didn't sleep most nights. When he did it was restless sleep—his mind haunted by the familiar nightmare that returned again and again. It was always the same. A long line of those who had died by his hand materialized slowly from the fog of his memory. In the thickest part of the night they returned, as he knew they would, as they did each night to march in single file through his mind, to stare through sightless, condemning eyes.

Once they had been good men, and now they were dead. Once they had laughed, and cried, and loved, and been loved. Now they only marched silently through his memory, and stared at him.

Lying on his hard bunk in the inky darkness, he had relived his whole life. It's funny what a man thinks about when he's convinced he's about to die. He thought of all the things in his life he wished he'd done and hadn't, or wished he'd done different.

He should have told his ma and pa he loved them instead of

just figuring they already knew. Why hadn't he taken longer to say goodbye? If he could only see them again, he would hug his ma like he knew she liked for him to. He would shake his pa's hand and feel the strength of that work hardened hand clasping his own. Why did I take all those things for granted?

He thought about Elizabeth Johnson, the only girl he had ever cared for. He remembered her long blonde hair with the curls on the ends that bounced and lifted in the breeze when she ran. In his mind he could almost see those sky-blue eyes that seemed to sparkle all the time.

He would never forget the way she had smiled at him at the box supper at the church in Sweetwater, Tennessee. She had laughed happily when he paid the last fifty cents he had for the apple pie she had brought. They had shared it together under the big old weeping willow tree down by the creek. Those times they met under the willow tree were some of the happiest memories of his life. They had made the spot their own special place. Those were good times, happy times.

He well remembered the day he left to join the cavalry. He'd ridden by the Johnson place to tell Elizabeth good-bye. He had never seen her look more beautiful. She had stretched high on her tiptoes to kiss him. The memory of the softness of her body when she brushed against him still tantalized him. He would never forget how she had yielded when he took her in his arms and surrounded her with a warm embrace. The picture in his mind of her tears as he mounted and rode away still hurt his heart.

She was the only girl he had ever kissed. Her lips tasted sweet, like a ripe strawberry. He had always kinda figured on marrying her someday. But all that was gone now, all gone.

A Cajun, the sergeant had said. What was his name? Boone? Yes, Boone LeFeve. Shiloh knew he would be no match for a professional knife fighter even if his arm were well, much less now. The others he had fought had known no more about knife fighting than he did. He had been lucky. But an experienced knife fighter? Shiloh knew he didn't have a prayer.

He listened to the other prisoners as they snored. Lester was the loudest of all. His bunk was right next to Shiloh's. He liked Lester. He was his best friend. Shiloh had hoped after the war they could be neighbors or something. Lester got on his nerves sometimes, but he was an okay guy.

The night was long and slow to die. Shiloh turned his head to stare through the door at the first blush of dawn. A new day was being born. Most likely my last. Well, if a man's got to die, guess one day's as good as another. Something gets born. Something dies. That's the way of it I guess. Well, he'd do what he had done with everything else in his life, he decided. He'd do his best. That was all a man could do.

The other prisoners avoided looking at him as they rousted out and tromped past his bunk on their way to breakfast. Again, he saw no point in making the effort. He never had learned to stomach watery grits and tasteless, weevil infested corn bread anyway, especially for breakfast.

"I'll try to slip you out a piece of pone if I can," Lester said, staring at him with a sad puppy dog look, like he was saying a last good-bye or something.

"Don't bother," Shiloh told him. "I'm not much hungry anyway."

Doc Williams limped in on his stiff leg just as Lester was leaving. The doc carried his little black bag in one hand and a large white rag in the other.

"How's that arm this morning?"

"It hurt all night."

"I don't wonder, that's a bad cut. Let me take a look at it."

The doc pulled a chair over close to Shiloh's bunk and lifted the wounded arm. For a long minute he stared at it. Without a word he snapped open his bag and took out a tin of foul smelling salve. He smeared the stuff over the wound and wrapped the arm tightly with a strip he tore off the big cloth.

"I heard about the fight today," the doc said sadly. "Wish there was something I could do. You ain't in no shape to fight."

"I'm obliged for what you've done, Doc."

"Here, let me tie this cloth around your neck for a sling. At least it'll keep that arm still so it won't start bleeding again."

The old doctor adjusted the large cloth and placed Shiloh's arm inside, then paused for a long moment and stared sadly before reaching a hand to pat Shiloh on the shoulder. A tiny silver tear escaped the old man's eye and inched its way along a deep wrinkle. He turned without a word and limped out the door.

Lester burst in and hurried to Shiloh's bunk. A big grin creased his boyish face as he pulled a square of cornbread from his coat pocket and proudly handed it to his friend.

"Here, I stole this for you slicker than a whistle. You need to eat it to keep up your strength. Everybody's talking about the fight. They're saying it's at ten o'clock this morning. I saw that Cajun fellow. He looks more like an Indian than a white man. He's bragging how he's gonna make short work of you. I told him that's what the other six thought too but now all they're doing is feeding the worms. He didn't like that too much. Hey, where'd you get the sling?"

"The doc came by and fixed it for me. Thanks for the pone."

"Good God Almighty!" Lester shouted and spun on his heels, hurrying for the door. "Seeing that sling give me an idea that might save your bacon. I'll be right back"

CHAPTER II

The sun broke clear and blazing hot; the weather had been that way for more'n a month. Lester made a beeline for the chow hall as fast as his legs could carry him. He hoped what he had seen earlier that morning was still there. Glancing quickly in both directions before ducking around the corner of the long wooden building, he dropped to his knees. Peering into the dim light underneath the elevated building, he swept his gaze along the ground. It was there.

Dropping to his belly he crawled slowly forward. He paused briefly to lick his lips and draw a deep breath before staring into the elliptical eyes of a four foot timber rattler, one of the most deadly snakes alive.

The big rattler fixed its evil looking eyes on Lester. Its head remained motionless as it slowly looped its thick body into a tight defensive coil. From that position, Lester knew it could strike with lightning speed. Experience had taught him its striking range would be about three feet.

The fully grown rattler was as big around as Lester's wrist. Its mouth opened wide and the forked tongue lashed out threateningly, testing the air. Curved fangs bared. The big rattlers on its tail played a chilling warning that would send shivers dancing up and down the spine of man and beast alike.

Inching slowly forward, Lester's stare locked on the big snake's nose. He would have only one chance. If he misjudged even a couple of inches, he would die. The rattler tightened his coil, a sure sign its strike would come at any instant. Its forked tongue flicked out. Beady eyes watched every move Lester made.

Slowly Lester stretched his armless sleeve far out to his left and inched it forward toward the snake. Sure enough, just like he hoped, the rattler's head swiveled slightly, following the empty sleeve. Cautiously, Lester moved his right hand into position.

Closer. Closer still. Another couple of inches and his hand would be in position.

A cold sweat broke across his face. Tears burned his eyes, blurred his vision, and trailed down his ruddy cheeks. His lips were suddenly dry. The only sound was his own heartbeat pounding in his chest and the steady rattled warning from the deadly snake. For a long moment that seemed like an eternity, time seemed to stand still.

Even though he was anticipating the strike, when it came, it still caught him by surprise. His heart skipped a beat. The frightening speed of the snake's attack was a blur of motion. One heartbeat it lay in a tightly wound coil, the next it was hurtling through the air toward Lester's outstretched arm. The poisonous fangs found their target and embedded deep into the empty sleeve of Lester's tattered army jacket.

Instantly, Lester's right hand shot out and locked on the scaly slickness just behind the snake's head. The big rattler's thick body struggled savagely, looping around Lester's arm. Its full body strength strained to free its head from the vice grip of Lester's hand.

"Settle down, Lucifer. I've got plans for you," Lester whispered, as he crawfished backwards out from under the floor, dragging the snake by his side.

He had to hurry. He knew the guards would be coming for

his friend any minute now. Holding the snake's head tightly, he slipped it under his coat and hurried toward the barracks. Shiloh still lay on his bunk, staring at the ceiling, when Lester entered.

"I've got a present for you," he told his friend, pulling the big rattler from under his coat.

"What the...where did you get that thing?"

"I caught it under the mess hall. It's a timber rattler, one of the most poisonous critters under the sun. This big fellow just might save your bacon today."

"How in the world did you manage to catch it without getting bit?"

"I've caught lots of 'em," Lester said proudly. "I used to catch 'em and sell 'em to the circuit preacher that come around every couple of months. The church my ma and pa went to believed that if you had enough faith you could handle poisonous snakes and even if you got bit, it wouldn't hurt you.

"The preacher and I had a secret agreement. He paid me fifty cents to catch one and milk the poison out of it just before he showed everybody how much faith he had, but he made a big mistake."

"What happened?" Shiloh asked, sensing that wasn't the whole story

"He quit paying and I quit milking," Lester said, chuckling at the memory.

"Just what am I supposed to do with that thing?" Shiloh wanted to know.

"Well, I figured we could hide it in your arm sling, kinda like a secret weapon. At the right time you just drag it out and give it a fling. If you're lucky enough to get old Lucifer on that Cajun he'll do the job for you. Even if you miss, maybe it'll distract him long enough to give you an opening. What do you think?"

"I think that's most likely the craziest thing I ever heard," Shiloh said, shaking his head. "But I don't reckon it makes a whole lot of difference which one does me in, the Cajun or the snake. How am I supposed to keep it from biting me?"

"Here," Lester said, stuffing the big rattler into the arm sling tail first. "Now slide your hand up against my hand. You have to keep a tight grip on it or it'll wiggle loose, then you won't have to worry about the Cajun. Scoot your hand down closer to its head. There...that's it. Now wrap your finger under its head and put your thumb on top so you can hold it's mouth shut. That way when you reach in to drag it out with your good hand it can't get its mouth open to get at you."

"This thing gives me the creeps," Shiloh complained. "It's wrapping itself around my arm."

"That just means it likes you, that's all," Lester said with a wry grin.

"Yeah, right."

"Hurry, I think I hear them coming. Let me make sure you can't see it—yeah, that looks good. Good luck, buddy. Don't forget, get it on him if you can."

The big sergeant of the guard stepped through the door followed closely by four of his men carrying rifles. They stomped across the room and positioned themselves on either side of Shiloh.

"Let's go, Reb," the Bear growled. "You know the routine."

Lester followed along behind as the little group made its way across the camp to the dry wash. Two plank walls had been built, closing off a section of the wash maybe thirty feet wide and forming, what the prisoners all called, 'the pit."

On either side of the wash, a small hill rose steeply forming a natural grandstand. On one hillside sat three hundred or so Confederate prisoners, all that had survived the winter. On the opposite side sat the Union guards, laughing and yelling, anxious for the upcoming fight. In the very center of the guards stood a large, upholstered chair. In the chair, smoking a cigar sat Colonel Samuel Mattox, Shiloh's sworn enemy.

The four guards escorting Shiloh stepped aside while the big sergeant pulled open a small gate. The sadistic giant leered happily as Shiloh ducked his head and stepped into the pen as he'd done on six previous occasions.

The searing mid morning sun cooked into the sandy bottom of the gully. Not a breath of air stirred. Shimmering heat waves radiated from the ground and drifted upward as if filtered from Hades itself. Shiloh squeezed his eyes to narrow slits to dull the blinding glare and peered at the man standing before him.

Boone Le Feve stood straight and tall in the very center of the pen. Like Lester said, the man looked more indian than white. His skin was the color of cooked sorghum and stretched taut over high cheekbones. His coal black, shoulder length hair was gathered together and tied. He was clean shaven except for a short, well trimmed mustache. A searching gaze from dark, penetrating eyes swept Shiloh from head to toe and back again. No trace of emotion showed on the man's face. Shiloh knew without a doubt he was staring into the face of a cold-blooded killer.

The sergeant stepped between them. He raised both hands high in the air, a gleaming, razor-sharp bayonet in each. It took a few minutes for the excited blue bellies to quiet down. In a loud, bullfrog, voice he boomed out.

"This here will be a no-holds-barred, fight to the finish. If either man quits before the other is dead, both will be shot. If the Cajun wins, he'll be set free. If Shiloh wins, well, I reckon he'll live to fight another day, but I figure the odds on that are mighty long." With that said, the sergeant dropped a bayonet at the feet of each man and made a hasty exit.

Shiloh bent to pick up his weapon, his eyes never leaving the Cajun. Before him stood a killer, one who, most likely had killed many times before. This man was a professional knife fighter. For a long moment the one called Boone Le Feve stood motionless, staring, his face expressionless. Then a quick flick of a booted toe and the blade sailed magically into his hand.

"So you are the one called Shiloh I hear so much talk about uh? I expected more." The Cajun said in a broken accent. "They say you have killed six men with the bayonet. I feel badly that you have only one arm. I have never killed a one armed man before."

Shiloh fixed a gaze on the man that stood before him. He saw a cruel smile that lifted one corner of the man's mouth, a mocking look in those coal-black eyes, a relaxed self-assurance in the Cajun's stance. Here is a fellow that is too sure of himself, it occurred to Shiloh.

In that moment, that instant of time, a dramatic change swept over him. Shiloh's knotted stomach seemed to relax. The restless twisting in his guts that started when he first learned who his opponent would be, now somehow stilled. A strange calmness settled over him.

Don't let it worry you none," Shiloh said evenly, "I've never killed a Cajun before, either."

"I could easily kill you right now from twenty feet away, you know," the Cajun bragged. "I could drive this blade through your heart with one flick of my hand before you could blink an eye. But no, I think that would be too quick, uh, too easy. I think they would like a little show. I think they would like to see me cut you up like a pig before you die, uh?"

"What are you gonna do?" Shiloh asked, trying to muster up a sound of confidence, "Talk me to death?"

"Ah, you are brave for one who is about to die," the Cajun said, replacing the smile on his face with a cold, blank, unemotional stare.

"You'll find I don't die so easy," Shiloh said.

Shiloh blotted all sound from his hearing. His eyes focused squarely upon his opponent, allowing no other movement to distract his attention. The two men approached each other, circling slowly, each with their eyes locked on the eyes of their opponent. Holding the bayonet out in front of his body, Shiloh dropped into a low stance, feet well apart, sliding along the ground, rather than lifting them, careful not to make a misstep, knowing one mistake would be his last. He figured the only chance he might have, and slim at best, was to catch the Cajun in a mistake.

Boone Le Feve was not only a professional, he was a show off. From his crouched stance he continually border-shifted the blade from one hand to the other.

He faked a quick lunge, then pulled it back, playing with his opponent. Shiloh didn't fall for the clumsy trick and continued to circle.

The Cajun flicked the bayonet to his left hand and made another lunge, this time following through. Shiloh sidestepped like a Mexican matador, allowing the point to pass mere inches from his belly. He countered with a quick backhand slash that made contact and opened a shallow cut on the Cajun's left arm.

"Oh, ho," the man said, "that was good, that was very good. Perhaps you will be a worthy opponent after all."

Suddenly the Cajun attacked with a fury. His right foot charging forward, again and again, followed by his left. Like a sword fighter he waded in, his bayonet slashing back and forth with ferocity scored in every movement, lunging first to the right, then to the left. Thrusting. Jabbing.

Shiloh could only back away against the onslaught, keeping his blade between them, warding off his opponent's probing attack. The metal of their weapons filled the little valley with a sharp ringing sound as they clashed.

Leaping aside, Shiloh lashed out with a booted foot, landing a vicious kick to the Cajun's right knee as he charged past. The man stumbled. For an instant the knee buckled, then recovered quickly before Shiloh could get to him.

Again they squared off and circled. Shiloh detected a change of expression on his opponent's face. Not fear, more like respect. Each man stalked his opponent, searching for an opening. Boone border-shifted his blade again and again, showing off despite his bleeding arm, putting on a show for the onlookers who were screaming for blood. The Cajun grew more cautious.

Shiloh decided his best defense might be a good offense. He tried a double slash, followed quickly by a triple, then a deep thrust. It proved to be a mistake. He felt a hot flush radiate up his arm. His right hand suddenly began tingling and went partially numb. His clutching fingers grew useless. The bayonet escaped his grasp and made a clanging sound when it hit the rocky ground.

"It is time to die, my friend," the Cajun snarled.

He lowered his knife slightly and slowly advanced. A devil's fire danced in his eyes. The killer's lips tugged into a wicked smile.

Shiloh glanced down at his wounded right hand. It hung loosely at his side. Blood streamed from a deep cut just above his wrist and dripped onto the sandy ground.

Then he remembered the snake. In the heat of the fight he had completely forgotten about the rattler. If there ever was a time to use the snake—his ace in the hole—this was it.

Could his fingers grasp the head of the snake? Did he have enough strength left in his hand to withdraw it without getting bit? What difference did it make? He was about to die anyway.

Shiloh deliberately turned his back to his opponent. At the same time he lifted his bleeding hand and reached inside the sling to close on the big rattler's warm head. He needed strength in his right hand and he needed it real sudden.

Calling on his energy reservoir one last time and draining it bone dry, he gripped with all the strength he could muster. In one sweeping motion he swept the snake from the white arm sling and wheeled around.

His arm arched sideways like a sling shot. The snake twisted in mid-flight as it hurtled toward the advancing Cajun.

Boone Le Feve froze in his tracks, his eyes rounded. A look of sheer terror washed across his face. The momentum of the reptile's flight wrapped its thick body around the Cajun's neck.

Shiloh watched as the huge mouth opened. Its head shot forward with lightening speed. Bared fangs sank deep into the side of the Cajun's throat.

The terrified man dropped his weapon. Both hands flew to the monster. He clawed. He tore at it, finally ripping it from his throat and flinging it from him, but it was too late.

A collective gasp swept across the crowd of spectators, followed by a chilling hush. Five hundred sets of eyes watched the gruesome scene being played out before them. A look of agonizing terror overtook the Cajun's face as Shiloh watched it turn a sickly shade of white. The doomed man's legs buckled, he sank to his knees in a dreamlike slowness as if about to pray.

For a long moment he knelt motionless, his face twisted with pain. A pitiful sounding groan escaped his tightly compressed lips. His eyes rounded with fear and pain. Searching, they found Shiloh's and the two men's stare locked for a long instant. Shiloh felt a moment of sympathy as he saw a desperate, pleading appeal for help reflected there. Then the Cajun's eyes went blank and walled white. He toppled face forward into the dirt.

The blue bellies who, only moments before, were screaming for a kill, now sat in stunned silence. For long moments an eerie hush hung over the little valley. The silence was suddenly shattered by a rider galloping through the front gate screaming at the top of his lungs.

"It's over! The war's over! General Lee has surrendered! It's over! The war's over! The North has won the war!"

Pure bedlam broke out. As one, both sides burst into shouts. Grown men hugged each other and jumped up and down, dancing around and around like young schoolgirls. Men dashed every which way, not knowing what to do, but so full of excitement they couldn't contain themselves.

Shiloh's gaze climbed the hillside to where the colonel sat. Their eyes met, and held for a moment, before the officer turned his head away abruptly, pushed himself from the chair, and strode hurriedly toward his headquarters building outside the fence.

In all the excitement, Shiloh was forgotten. He tore a strip of cloth from his arm sling and wrapped it tightly around his new cut to slow the bleeding. As he stooped to scoop up the Cajun's bayonet, his eyes caught movement along the ground. The big rattler slithered off toward a crevice in the side of the dry wash.

"Go ahead, big fellow," Shiloh whispered aloud. "I reckon we both earned our freedom here today."

Colonel Samuel Mattox tore angrily from his seat and stomped toward his office. All around him men were shouting, laughing, crying, overcome with the news that the war was finally over. They would be going home.

For Colonel Sam Mattox, it was anything but good news. He had no home. The only home he could remember was an orphanage, or one of the half dozen reform schools he had been in and out of. The closest thing to a family he had ever known was a gang on the south side of Chicago called the Devil's Disciples, and the army. The army had been his pick of only two choices given him after being convicted of armed robbery.

"It's the Illinois State Penitentiary or the army," the stern faced Judge had said.

Sam quickly discovered his gang experience could actually help him in his army career. The way to climb the proverbial chain of command ladder was exactly the same: outsmart, overpower or destroy the one directly above you and the position was usually yours. He had used all three methods in his climb to the rank of colonel. All that, only to have his career destroyed by this nobody they called Shiloh. Now, even his efforts to do away with this young upstart had been thwarted.

By promising freedom, a promise he had no intention of keeping, to any Confederate prisoner who could defeat Shiloh, he had hoped to be rid of this Johnny Reb once and for all. Yet in seven fight-to-the-death matches in a 'battle of the bayonets,' this lowly cavalry captain had somehow been victorious in each one. Well, the games were over. He'd see that Shiloh never walked out of this camp alive.

Another courier galloped through the gate and reined up on a lathered bay just as the colonel stepped onto the porch. The young soldier lighted from his mount, saluted smartly, and held out a leather message pouch.

"Colonel Mattox, sir," the soldier said, holding his salute, waiting for it to be returned. "It's an urgent message from General Halleck, sir. I'm ordered to wait for a reply."

"Very well, soldier," the colonel said, briefly touching a gloved finger to the brim of his hat in a lazy salute. "See to your mount and report back here in fifteen minutes. I'll post my reply."

"Yes, sir," the courier replied, again saluting.

The colonel ignored the last salute; he found the ritual boring. He glanced only briefly at his men, still engaged in their revelry at the news of the war's end, then strode quickly into his private office and closed the door.

Slouching down behind his desk, he teethed off his gloves and opened the mail pouch. Most likely the official notification of the surrender, he figured. He unfolded the paper and read.

TO: COLONEL SAMUEL MATTOX
COMMANDER, CAMP DOUGLAS PRISONER OF WAR CAMP

THIS IS TO ADVISE YOU THAT ALL CONFEDERATE

PRISONERS OF WAR ARE TO BE RELEASED IMMEDIATELY. CAMP DOUGLAS IS TO BE CLOSED AND ALL RECORDS TRANSFERRED TO HEADQUARTERS FOR REVIEW AND AUDITING.

FURTHER, ALL TROOPS UNDER YOUR COMMAND ARE TO REPORT TO ALTON HEADQUARTERS FORTHWITH FOR REASSIGNMENT OR DISCHARGE.

Signed: Major General Henry Halleck
Commanding General, Bureau of Prisons

For a few long minutes he sat unmoving, stunned by the message. His mind whirled. What would he do? If they audited his records they were sure to find discrepancies. They would discover he had been stealing from the accounts. Questions would be asked. Likely another court martial. This time it would mean prison, or worse. He could not allow that to happen.

He hurried across the office to bolt the door, then went to the heavy safe in the corner. Kneeling, he spun the twin dials to the combination known only to him, twisted the handle, and swung the door open.

For several long moments he stared transfixed at the stacks of money. Reaching a hand he removed one of several bundles and allowed his thumb to fan the edge of the thick packet of bills, a small fortune. Money diverted from food, medicine, and other accounts allocated for the care of the Confederate prisoners under his charge.

Now, this too, would be gone, he lamented. If the stupid war could have lasted just one more year Sam Mattox would have been fixed for life. Well, no use crying over spilt milk. He would just have to find another way. First though, he had to cover his tracks.

A fire? Sure! Why not? Plumes of black smoke were already

billowing from fires set by the celebrating prisoners. He would torch his headquarters and blame it on the prisoners. All the records would be destroyed.

Snatching a pair of saddlebags from a nearby wall peg he hurriedly scooped the money from the safe to the saddlebags. He purposely left the safe door wide ajar and strew the remaining papers and account books haphazardly around the office.

Sweeping a long glance, he was pleased. A good fire that could be blamed on the prisoners would do the trick.

Turning on his heels he stalked from the room, careful to lock the door behind him. He didn't want anyone stumbling in and discovering his preparation before he had everything set. At the appropriate time he would have a couple of his trusted men torch the place after the rest had pulled out.

Shiloh, Lester, and Doc Williams sat at a table in the deserted chow hall. After the guards abandoned the camp and withdrew outside the fence, the prisoners went on a rampage. They quickly took what little food remained in the mess hall and storage shed, stole anything of value, and destroyed the rest. Black smoke billowed skyward from a dozen fires. Only Lester's threatening presence prevented the prisoners from torching the dining hall too.

"I fetched the little chest from under your bunk and that beat up old cavalry hat you're so fond of before they burned our barracks," Lester said as he watched the doctor sewing up Shiloh's wrist.

"Thanks," Shiloh breathed through clenched teeth.

"It's a good thing the war's over," Doc said, bending low over his work, "I'm already sewing stitches on top of stitches."

"What's happening outside?" Shiloh asked Lester. "You best keep a sharp eye or they'll burn this place down around our ears."

"Naw," Lester drawled, pulling himself up from the bench along the table to head for the door. "The guards are too busy celebrating and getting ready to pull out and the prisoners have already had their fun. All they want to do now is go home, they're already bunching around the front gate."

"Where're you headed, Doc?" Shiloh asked.

"Don't rightly know. I reckon I'll go back to Arkansas. Don't know any place else. Don't rightly know why though, ain't anybody there to go back to. How about you?"

"I'm gonna head back to Tennessee. Once a man gets those Smoky Mountains in his mind, there just ain't room left to think of much else. Besides, I got family there. My ma and pa will be expecting me and I've got a powerful lonesome to see them."

"Now that would be nice, having somebody waiting on you, I mean."

"Hey, Doc, why don't you come with me and Lester? Folks get sick in the Tennessee Mountains too, though not as much as other places, I reckon. You could doctor in Tennessee just as good as you could in Arkansas. Besides, I might need some more sewing done.

"My pa's got a whole section of the best farmland in the Tennessee Valley and there's lots of folks scattered around you could see to. How about it, Doc, will you come go with us."

"Hadn't thought none on it but . . .well . . ..can't think of any reason why not," the Doctor told him, tying off the last stitch.

"Good, then it's settled. We best get started pretty quick. We can get in a half days' walking before dark."

"Shiloh!" Lester called out from the door. "The Bear's coming with a whole squad of armed guards."

"What could he want now?" Doc Williams asked, closing his black bag with a snap and pushing stiffly to his feet.

"Probably couldn't stand leaving without saying good-bye," Shiloh said sarcastically.

The big sergeant stomped through the door, followed closely by eight heavily armed guards. One look at the man's face and Shiloh knew it wasn't good-bye he had come to say.

A wide smile pushed the evil guard's whiskers apart, revealing yellow tobacco stained, rotting teeth. It was the first time Shiloh could ever remember seeing the sergeant of the guard smiling.

"We been waiting for you to show up at the gate," the man growled. "We couldn't wait no longer."

"Aw, you didn't have to wait on my account," Shiloh said mockingly.

"Let's go. The colonel don't like to be kept waiting."

Two guards grabbed both of Shiloh's arms and held him while another tied his hands behind his back. The guards used their rifles to shove him toward the door as the sergeant led the way.

A few prisoners cast inquiring looks as the guards pushed Shiloh past a knotted group that had congregated near the gate, waiting for it to open. As the big sergeant approached they dropped their gaze to stare at the ground, not wanting to get involved. They didn't care about anything except putting the notorious prison camp behind them. They looked like walking skeletons. Many limped badly on frostbitten feet from the previous winter, hardly able to pull themselves along. A few were being half carried by fellow prisoners. All had expressionless, zombie stares fixed in their eyes.

Colonel Samuel Mattox sat atop his black gelding outside the gate like royalty, puffing on a long cigar. He was a sight to behold, sure enough. His blue officer's dress uniform was spotless and pressed flawlessly. Its brass buttons shined like polished gold. A battle sword hung from a sash draped over his shoulder and rested against his left side. A flapped holster was strapped to his right hip. Black, highly polished, high-top boots captured the afternoon sun and reflected it off into nothingness.

"You didn't really think I would let you just walk away, did you?" he asked, fixing Shiloh with a hard stare. A smirking, faked smile wrinkled his face.

"The war's over, Colonel," Shiloh told him, staring up at the man whose face suddenly twisted with hatred. "Your side won."

"No sir! No sir!" the Colonel screamed, his face turning beet red. "The war will never be over until one of us is dead."

The officer gave a quick nod of his head. Shiloh cut a glance toward the sergeant of the guard. He held a heavy rope in his hand. It had been fashioned into a noose. A surge of understanding swept through Shiloh; they were going to hang him.

Taking a couple of steps toward the gate, the cruel sergeant tossed the noose over the crossbar. Two guards drag Shiloh forward and held him underneath the dangling noose. A third guard slipped the loop over his head and slid the knot tight below his left ear. Shiloh watched in horrified awareness as the sergeant held the loose end and looked up at the colonel.

"Goodbye, Shiloh," the officer said, and nodded his head.

Instinctively, he sucked short puffs of air through clenched teeth as he felt the noose tightening, lifting him off his feet. A tortured growl shredded his throat as the words surged up from his soul.

"I'll see you in...!" Shiloh's angry scream climbed from deep inside his being and burst from his throat. The cry reverberated across the rolling hills before the words were choked off and he dangled helplessly.

CHAPTER III

They wanted to scream out, to plead for their friend's life. Instead, all Lester and Doc Williams could do was stand by helplessly and watch. They both knew there was nothing they could do. They watched anxiously until the colonel and his men rode away, then rushing forward, untied the rope and gently lifted Shiloh to the ground.

"He's still alive," the Doc pronounced, lifting his ear from Shiloh's chest, "but just barely. Here, Lester, help me. When I motion to you, push real hard on his chest. We've got to hurry, he's already turning purple."

Hurriedly loosening the slipknot, they removed the rope. Doc pried open his friend's mouth and placing his own mouth against Shiloh's purpling lips, blew into the mouth as hard as he could and at the same time motioned for Lester to push.

Several long minutes passed. The two worked feverishly. Finally, Shiloh coughed and began a rattled breathing on his own. Hearing the sound of hoofbeats returning, they half carried, half dragged Shiloh to a small clump of scrub oak bushes nearby where Doc could examine their friend closer.

"He's got a ruptured larynx," Doc Williams pronounced after examining Shiloh for several minutes. Doc gazed down gravely and sadly shook his head. "I probably ought to do a tracheotomy, but that would mean he'd never talk again. He's struggling, but he's still able to get some air through. I'm gonna hold off for now."

"What's a . . .whatever that was you said?" Lester asked.

"It's where I would cut a hole in his throat and put a little tube in the hole so he could breath through it. I've done it lots of times."

"But if you did, you say he wouldn't be able to talk?"

"No, but he'd be alive."

"Don't know how he'd feel about it," Lester said. "It was me, if I couldn't talk I might just as well be dead."

"Hold on," the doc said. "He's coming around."

The two watched anxiously as Shiloh's eyes slowly tugged open to narrow slits. He blinked, as if trying to clear the darkness away. Lester stared into the pale green eyes of his friend he had known for over a year, and hardly recognized the man he saw there. Something was different about him.

His eyes—they had a blank look about them. They stared fixedly, but seemed to see nothing. Those eyes of his now burned with a look of hatred so intense a chill shot up Lester's spine and he quickly looked away, terrified by what he saw.

Awareness returned gradually to Shiloh's mind, releasing him grudgingly from his surreal state. A blood hazed curtain swam before his eyes. He heard a loud, rattled breathing, and was shocked to discover it was his own. His lungs begged for more air; each gasping breath became a life-threatening struggle. He wheezed down a ragged draught of air and struggled for more.

Each tiny intake sweet and precious but never enough to satisfy his starving lungs. Something was blocking the air's passage.

Where am I? His mind screamed out. What has happened to me? Am I alive?

The vague outline of two forms hovered over him. Their images skewed and trembling. Recognition came slowly. His lips moved, mouthing silent questions. Nothing came out but a hoarse rattling.

"Don't try to talk," A familiar voice cautioned. "Your throat has been damaged. It'll take some time to heal."

The reality of what had happened crept over him and with it, a molten fury boiled deep within him such as he'd never known before. He felt possessed by an all consuming hatred he wouldn't have believed he was capable of. *This isn't the end of it, Colonel!* He swore to himself. *Somehow, sometime, I'll set things right if it takes me until the end of time.*

His hands went to his throat. The touch brought a stab of added pain. His throat was swollen to near twice its normal size.

"Let's get him down to that little stream yonder," the doc said.

Shiloh felt Lester's hand slide under his shoulders and lift. The world spun crazily. He had to get up and the task seemed impossible. Then he staggered between his two friends, his arms around their shoulders.

He saw the water and collapsed to his knees, plunging his head beneath the soothing wetness. The water felt heavenly. Its coolness softened the hurt and cleared the tangled cobwebs from his mind. He gulped a greedy mouthful and choked as he tried to swallow. The water refused to go down. Fear swept over him. Near panic overwhelmed him. He couldn't swallow and could hardly breathe!

"It'll come, son," the doc said. "Give it time. Tilt your head back and let it trickle down your throat a little at a time."

He did. The harshness of the cool water burned his throat, but quenched his blinding thirst.

"There was nothing we could do," Lester said. His voice quivering and pleading for his friends understanding and forgiveness. "They just laughed and rode away."

Shiloh nodded his head and reached to squeeze his friend's arm understandingly. His eyes closed. An inky darkness enveloped him. He was so tired.

* * *

They spent the night by the little stream. A new sense of foreboding arrived with the dawn. Shiloh blinked the world into a fuzzy focus. A moment of frantic helplessness captured him as he struggled for every breath and couldn't swallow.

Doc examined the swollen throat, which had now turned a purplish-blue. The water slid down better though and felt cool and refreshing. A deep, raw rope burn ringed Shiloh's throat.

"It's just gonna take time," the doc said. "I've done all I can do. You're gonna have an ugly scar where that rope did its worst, I'm afraid."

"Do you feel up to walking?" Lester asked. "Or should we stay here awhile longer?"

Shiloh felt daunted by the journey that lay before them, especially in his condition. But he knew they were a long way from Tennessee and walking was the only hope they had of getting there. He answered Lester's question by pushing unsteadily to his feet. He clamped his battered old Confederate cavalry hat on his head, scooped up the little wooden chest containing the seven bayonets, and struck out due south. His friends hurried to keep up.

They moved steady all morning. Doc hop-stepped along on his crippled leg and somehow managed to keep up. They stopped often to allow Shiloh to regain his strength. Lester kept up a stream of one-sided conversation, seemingly not needing, nor expecting an answer.

By noon Shiloh and Doc knew Lester's entire history from the time he could walk to the present. Every once in awhile Doc offered a comment or an "Is that so?" This seemed to only encourage Lester to expound further.

"You fellas see that farm house up ahead?" Lester asked, lifting his only arm to point as if it were a rifle. "I'm gonna get us something to eat. I ain't had anything fit to eat in so long, I'm having to apologize to my stomach."

"We're in Yankee country," Doc reminded him. "They ain't gonna feed three Johnny Rebs just let out of a prison camp. What's the matter with you?"

"Now you just look at us," Lester said, walking backwards in front of them so he could look them in the eyes. "We got a man that can't talk, a man that can't walk, and a fellow with just one arm. Even a Yankee ain't cold-hearted enough to turn us down."

"You're liable to get yourself a load of buckshot in your behind is what you're likely to get," Doc told him, slanting a critical look in Lester's direction.

"Naw. They'll feed us, you just wait and see. I can talk a condemned man outta his last meal."

Shiloh and Doc stopped a safe distance away at a split rail fence that surrounded the bare, flat board house. Lester tromped right up the path toward the house as if he'd lived there his whole life.

"Hello in the house!" he hollered as he stomped loudly up the steps onto the porch.

"Wouldn't surprise me none if that boy just opened the door and went right on in," Doc commented as they watched. "When he has to, that boy can use ten dollar words like they were a nickle a dozen."

The door opened a crack and the twin nose of a double-barreled shotgun poked through. Lester stopped in his tracks and pushed his one arm out between them, palm raised. Shiloh and Doc couldn't hear the exchange of words but Lester was shore doing some fast talking. He half turned and pointed to his two companions standing outside the fence.

A woman, with graying hair pulled tight into a bun, poked her head where the shotgun had been and peered a long minute at the two men by the fence. The door slowly creaked open and the shotgun disappeared. The elderly woman stepped through the door and spent another half minute looking Lester up and down, then pointed to the edge of the porch and went back inside.

Lester beckoned with his arm, inviting them forward, then sat himself down, leaned his back against a post, and creased his face with a self-satisfying smile.

"Well if that don't beat all," Doc muttered through a wide grin as he hurried toward the porch.

Lester beamed proudly as Shiloh and Doc approached and planted themselves on the edge of the porch.

Shiloh reached a hand to pat his friend on the shoulder and nod his head in appreciation.

"I gotta give you credit, Lester," Doc said. "I reckon I underestimated you. 'Course, as much practice as you get talking, I reckon it just follows you oughtta be right good at it."

"It's my puppy dog eyes," Lester bragged, leaning back, obviously pleased with himself. "Women just can't resist 'em."

Turned out the lady was a widow woman who called herself grandma Venable. The greens and hog jowl she brought out looked and smelled delicious, and if the way Lester and Doc was going after it was any measure, it must have been. Between bites, Lester explained to the woman why Shiloh wasn't eating his and smiled appreciatively when Shiloh forked his food onto Lester's plate.

Without a word the widow went back in the house and returned with a whole fruit jar of canned tomatoes. Shiloh offered a grateful smile and tipped the jar to his lips. The zesty aroma made his mouth water and his cheeks hurt. He sipped the salty juice slowly, allowing it to slide down his swollen throat. It burned his throat something awful, but he had never in his life tasted anything so good.

They thanked the nice lady again and again and turned to wave as they strode through the gate and back onto the road. She lifted a hand, turned, and disappeared into the house.

Managing another six or eight miles before dark, they decided to spend the night beside a pretty little creek. They all spent a half hour or so in the waist deep water scrubbing away some of the filth accumulated between once a month baths they were allowed in the prison camp.

"Maybe I won't have to sleep downwind of you tonight, Lester," Doc told him, dipping his head and scrubbing his wet hair.

"If I can stand the sound of your snoring, you ought not be griping about the smell," Lester replied. "I swear, I never heard anybody snore so loud. You'd wake the dead."

"Now that's the pot calling the kettle black," Doc shot back.

Shiloh liked hearing the two good friends joshing one another. He squatted down in the water up to his nose, allowing the cool liquid to bathe his neck. The swelling seemed to be subsiding some.

They finally climbed out, hung their wet clothes on nearby bushes, and sat shivering and staring into the little fire Lester had coaxed into life with the matches widow Venable had given them.

"Boy, a cup of coffee shore would go down good," Doc said, poking the fire absently with a stick and watching the sparks drift upward.

"It's been so long since I had a cup I've near forgotten what it tastes like," Lester agreed.

"I ain't," Doc assured him.

"Shore seems funny you not being able to say nothing," Lester said, aiming a look in Shiloh's direction.

"You talk enough for you and him both," Doc told him.

"How long you reckon before he'll be able to talk, Doc?" Lester asked.

"Hard to say. Maybe when the swelling goes down, maybe never."

Shiloh lay back near the fire and stared up at a million twinkling stars punching light holes in the velvety black curtain like distant fireflies. The moon was full and close, it seemed a man could just reach out and touch it.

It was a peaceful silence broken only by the shiver of windblown leaves and the constant chirping of crickets. A swarm of memories flooded his mind. Sadness tugged at him. Hatred gnawed at his insides, a festering sore. He squeezed his eyes shut, trying to shut off the bitter thoughts.

He was on his way home, which ought to count for something. How long had it been since he told ma and pa good-bye, climbed on his horse, and rode off to war? He had left the day he turned eighteen, April 18, 1861. It's been four years. Sure will be good to see them again.

Shiloh actually slept a dreamless sleep that night for the first time since he didn't know when. The marching dead had not followed him to this place. But he dared not hope he had entered a time of grace or forgiveness.

They were up and moving by sunup. Shiloh figured they would be doing good if they made ten or twelve miles a day on foot. At that rate, it would take them most of two months to get home.

Twice that day they met wagons, and one fellow on horseback. Each time they were eyed suspiciously. Shiloh couldn't help noticing how close the folks kept their hands to their guns as they passed. Late that afternoon they saw a farmhouse a little ways off the road down a narrow lane.

"Let's walk on down and say a howdy," Lester said. "Maybe I can get us something to eat. Them tomatoes are good but they just don't fill a man's stomach up much."

Shiloh just shook his head as Lester turned down the wagon-rutted lane toward the house. Lester led the way, Shiloh and Doc followed along behind. It was a small place, maybe three rooms, and looked awfully rundown. A dilapidated looking old barn and chicken house stood nearby.

Before Lester got a stones throw of the house a thin looking fellow in overalls and carrying a shotgun stepped from the house onto the porch.

"That's far enough," he hollered in a gruff voice. "Don't you come no closer. I done chased one of you Rebs off yesterday. Git off my place! I don't want you around here."

"We don't mean you no harm, mister," Lester hollered back. "All we wanted was a drink of water and maybe a cold biscuit."

"I done told you once, won't tell you again. You gray coat Rebels ain't getting nothing around here. You want water, go to the creek with the rest of the animals. Go on! Get outta here before I dust your britches."

"Come on Lester," Doc told him. "Let's go on down the road before that fella shoots you."

Lester stood unmoved for another long minute, challenging, seemingly unwilling to accept that the man wouldn't even allow them a drink of water. The farmer jerked the shotgun to his shoulder and fired a blast into the air over Lester's head. "I said git!"

It was clear Lester was fuming, but he turned and stomped past Shiloh and Doc, mumbling under his breath, and headed on down the road, mad as all get out.

"That fellow had no call to do that," he complained to himself. "No call at all. He ain't a lick better than us."

Three more miles or so down the road they came to a creek and decided to stop for the night. Leaving the road, they walked a quarter mile into the woods before stopping in a little grove of elm trees.

"We ought to be far enough off the road so a fire won't attract attention," Doc said.

Lester was still pouting about the way the farmer treated them and didn't bother to reply. Shiloh just nodded his head in agreement and made his way down to the sloping creek bank. He squatted and cupped a handful of water and brought it to his thirsty lips. Tipping his head back to let the water run down his throat, he was surprised when he felt himself swallow.

I can swallow! He thought. An avalanche of excitement swept over him. If I can swallow, maybe I can talk, too! He swallowed again and hesitantly mouthed a single word.

"Maybe," came out in a dry, raspy whispered sound, but it was understandable. He wheeled and hurried back up the bank and stopped in front of Doc like a young schoolboy bringing an apple to the teacher.

"I...can...talk," he forced his words out.

Doc's face lit up like a spring morning. He slapped his bum leg with the palm of a hand.

"By cracky you shore can!" he said excitedly.

Lester rushed over to Shiloh, patting him on the back like he was burping a baby. Wide smiles and back patting occupied the next several minutes.

Lester gathered the makings for a fire while Doc examined Shiloh's throat. After Lester had given birth to a crackling fire, he headed back toward the road without so much as a "by your leave."

"Where you off to?" Doc hollered after him. To which Lester only lifted a hand and disappeared into the woods.

"Wonder where he thinks he's going?" Doc Williams said.

Shiloh just shook his head and shrugged. He and Doc sat around the little fire and talked. Doc mostly did the talking but Shiloh kept experimenting with his newfound voice. It seemed like the more he tried, the more understandable his whispered words got.

"How long before I can talk normal?" he asked the doc.

Firelight drew a jagged circle and filled their campsite with an amber glow. The silence of the night was broken only be the constant sound of crickets and the occasional call of a whippoorwill. For a long space Doc didn't answer, he just stared at the flames like he hadn't heard the question.

"Doc?" Shiloh whispered hoarsely.

"I heard you, son," the doc said, still seemingly hypnotized by the flames of the campfire. "I was just trying to figure out how to say the words. I'm just a country doctor and I shore don't know everything, mind you. I'd rather take a whipping than to have to tell you this and I'd give might near anything to find out I'm wrong, but I don't reckon you'll ever talk much better than you are right now.

"I know your throat is still swelled and it's hard to tell, but reach your finger and touch your Adams apple. Go ahead," the doc told him.

Shiloh did as his friend suggested. He touched his throat where his Adams apple should have been, but there was nothing there. It had disappeared.

"What happened to it?" he whispered sadly.

"That noose was so tight around your throat and as big as you are, your weight caused that heavy rope to rupture your larynx."

Doc Williams circled his fingers into the palm of his hand forming a loose fist.

"The larynx, some folks call it the voice box, is a sort of tube made out of tough cartilage, kind of like my hand. Inside this tube are two fibrous sheets of tissue called the vocal cords. When air from your lungs pass across these cords they make sounds. Our tongue, palate, and lips form these sounds into what we call words. That's how we say things.

"The problem is, son, when that rope crushed your larynx, it also damaged your vocal cords, most likely tore them might near in two. They ain't apt to ever grow back like they were. Like I said, I figure you're talking about as good as you'll ever talk."

Shiloh was stunned by what his friend told him. How can I go around talking in a raspy whisper the rest of my life? He dropped his head and stared forlornly into the fire for a long time.

It was awhile before they heard somebody coming through the woods lickety-split. Shiloh sure hoped it was Lester. It was. He trotted into the circle of firelight all out of breath and holding a chicken by it's feet. It's head had been wrung off.

"We're gonna have us a chicken to roast," Lester announced proudly.

"Don't tell me. Let me guess," Doc said. "That Yankee back yonder is gonna be one chicken short come morning."

"I shore do reckon so, Doc," Lester said, pulling feathers as fast as he could.

It was near midnight before the chicken was good done, but it was well worth the wait.

"Lester," Doc said between bites, "you could have got yourself shot doing it, but this shore is good chicken."

"Reckon it's as good as I ever ate," Shiloh whispered, nodding his head in agreement.

"Your talking pretty good there, partner," Lester said.

"You're gonna have to get use to me whispering though," Shiloh told him. "Doc says this is about as good as I'll ever talk."

"So?" Lester said, "We'll just have to listen closer."

Shiloh's restless dreams returned that night, the same as always. Out of the foggy dregs of his memory emerged the familiar line of marching dead. Their glassy, sightless eyes stared at him in condemnation. Silently they marched an ever tightening circle around him—nightmares disguised as memories.

Their faces were familiar. Some he had known. Others he had never seen before they met in the life or death struggle for the entertainment of the colonel and his Union guards. They were simply desperate men willing to risk death for a chance to be set free from the camp of death. There were seven of them, all former fellow prisoners.

Shiloh had taken the life of scores of men during the many battles of the 'brother against brother' war, but those were different. That was war. Somehow these seven were different. He had killed them all right, but their blood was on the colonel's hands too.

The pale gray light of coming day found them up and on the road trudging south. They wanted to put as many tracks as possible between them and that Yankee farmer before he discovered he was missing a chicken.

"He's so dumb he'll think a fox got it," Lester told them.

"Yeah, but this fox only had two legs and one arm," Doc said.

They walked steady, eating up the miles. They traveled through sweeps of forested plateaus where expanses of spring-green trees rustled in the wind. They passed through countryside knobby with rolling hills and creased with wooded valleys. Anticipation grew with every footfall. Each step took them closer home.

By mid afternoon the sky began to get ugly. A line of dark, angry looking clouds were building off in the west. A distant rumbling began to draw steadily closer and louder and gave warning of the storm to come. The wind shifted, bringing the pungent, unmistakable smell of rain washed air. They needed to find some kind of shelter fast.

The first gust of wind-driven rain hit them with a fury, lashing at them, soaking them to the skin. A golden chain of lightening cracked from one horizon to the other. They leaned into the driving rain and plodded on down the muddy wagon road.

Though well before nightfall, the storm had cloaked their world in darkness. Peering through the pounding rainstorm, Shiloh caught sight of the faintest twinkle of light up ahead. It was a farmhouse.

Lamplight filtered through a front window and made a welcome sight. A crackling streak of lightning shot across the sky, lighting the area like day and revealing a nearby barn. With a waving point of his arm Shiloh headed for it.

It was a sprawling structure with a wagon-size hallway down the middle. One whole side was lined with individual horse stalls. It smelled of horse manure, saddle leather, and fresh hay. It was dry and comfortable and would make a good place to ride out the storm. Through the flash of lightening Lester spotted a ladder nailed to one side of the hallway that led to a hayloft. He bounded up it with his one hand like a squirrel.

"Hey," he called back down, "come on up. We found us a poor man's hotel."

Shiloh and Doc climbed the ladder and found Lester sprawled out, spreading his full inches on a mattress of soft, sweet smelling hay. They joined him. Shiloh shared what was left of his jar of tomatoes. Then they lay back, listened to the pounding rain on the sheet-iron roof above their heads, and quickly drifted off to a sound sleep.

He thought it a dream when he heard the scream. Instantly Shiloh was awake. He listened intently. Long moments passed. Again it came, shattering the stillness of the night. It was a woman's scream. A long, high-pitched, hurting scream, followed by short spasmodic cries. Doc and Lester heard it too and were already up and crawling toward the ladder.

The violent storm had passed and left a steady downpour in its wake.

Rain pelted them as they rushed from the barn and trotted toward the source of the hurting woman. A light from the farmhouse cast a square pattern of orange on a wide front porch.

Another piercing, heart wrenching plea for help came from the house as Shiloh leaped from the ground to the porch in one jump. Two running steps brought him to the door. He pushed. It flung open. His quick sweeping glance showed him two small children, a boy and a girl, cowing in a corner. Their faces masked with fear. Tears streamed down their cheeks. Great sobs wracked their small bodies. The boy, no more than five or six, held his younger sister close in his protecting arms.

"Where?" Shiloh shouted a single word.

The boy raised a hand to point at a closed door to another room. Shiloh bounded across the room, followed closely by Lester and Doc.

The door gave way to his push. Again he raked the room with a searching glance. The source of the agony was a young looking woman in the bed. Her knees were drawn up near her waist. Blood covered both her and the rumpled bedclothes.

A young man bending over the bed twisted a look. A terrified expression distorted his face. Pleading eyes told the whole story.

"Doc!" Shiloh mouthed a raspy yell. "Get in here fast!"

One quick look was all doc needed as he rushed through the door.

"Lester," he said calmly. "Heat me lots of water and make it snappy. Shiloh, find me some rags and lots of 'em. This woman's trying to have a baby."

"What's wrong?" the pleading husband asked, not knowing nor seeming to care who these men were.

Doc shrugged out of his soaking-wet jacket and quickly rolled up his sleeves even as he was examining the woman.

"Looks like the baby's breach," Doc said to no one and everyone. Hold on to her hands. She's gonna need all the support she can get."

"There was already hot water on the stove," Lester said, dragging a small table near the foot of the bed and sitting a big dishpan full of steaming hot water on it.

Shiloh rushed in with an armload of towels and sheets. The

woman's screams were tearing his heart out by the roots. He spun
on his heels and followed Lester into the front room to escape the
sight of the suffering.

Lester knelt in front of the two frightened children. In soft
words he patiently explained that the fellow with them was a
doctor and he was going to do everything he could to help their
mother get well again.

"What's your name?" he asked the boy who still had his arms
around his sister. She clung tightly to him and buried her face
against his chest when anyone looked her way.

"J . . .Johnny," the boy managed to get out between stuttering
sobs. "Is my ma gonna die?"

"You're ma is gonna be just fine," Lester tried to assure the
boy. "What's your sister's name?"

"Kate," the boy said.

"Well, my name's Lester. That ugly fellow over there
is called Shiloh. We're here to help your ma if we can.
How old are you, Johnny?"

"I'm going on six."

"Six years old?" Lester acted surprised. "Well, I could tell
you were near growed up. I'll bet you help your pa with the chores
too, don't you?"

"Y-yes sir."

"Now, you see there. I knowed you was growed up. You have
to be big to do chores. How old are you Kate?"

"I...I'm...four." the frightened little girl choked out, snubbed
as she said the words.

"Really? How'd you get so pretty in just four years? You
know what? I'll bet you look just like your ma don't you?

The birthing of a smile tugged at the little girl's lips as she
swiped the tears with her dress sleeve and nodded her head.

"I swear to my time," Lester said. "Is that a coffee pot I see
over yonder? I'll bet your pa and the doctor would shore like to

have a cup of coffee when they get through doctoring your ma. I'm not real shore I remember how to make a pot of coffee. You suppose the two of you could show me so we could make up a pot?"

Shiloh paced the floor nervously and watched Lester and the two children hurrying around the kitchen making a pot of coffee. The screams had quieted down some. Only a low moan reached his ears now and then. Suddenly it got real quiet and his heart did a flip-flop. What could be going on? Had something bad happened?

The silence was broken by the sound of a hand striking bare skin. Then a baby's first gasping cry. The next few minutes seemed like an hour. Finally, the door opened and the kid's pa strode proudly into the front room carrying a newborn baby wrapped in a small blanket. A huge smile occupied the man's face.

"It's a boy," the new father announced. "Johnny, Kate, you've got a new little brother."

Both kids rushed over as their father squatted down to give them their first look.

"How's your wife?" Shiloh asked anxiously. "Is she gonna be okay?"

"The doctor says she'll be in bed for awhile but she's gonna be fine."

Shiloh allowed himself a relieved smile and strolled over to get a look at the new baby.

"His name is Andy. Named after his grandfather Andrew," the new father said proudly. Then, sticking out a hand. "By the way, I'm John Walters. I just met Doctor Williams."

"Good to meet you, Mr. Walters. They call me Shiloh. That's Lester over there stirring up a pot of coffee. Hope you don't mind."

"Not at all. I could use a cup and I'm sure the doctor could. He's a real good doctor. If you fellows hadn't come along when you did..."

The door opened and Doc walked into the room rolling down his sleeves and swiping sweat from his face with a clean towel.

"She's doing good," he announced, striding over to take another look at the baby. "Your wife lost a lot of blood but she's a mighty strong young lady. She's resting now, she'll be fine in a week or so. Is that coffee I'm smelling?"

"It shore is, Doc," Lester replied happily. "Miss Kate and Johnny here, they figured you and Mr. Walters could use a cup so they made a pot for you."

"Don't reckon I've smelled anything so good since I don't know when," Doc said, scraping out a chair at the kitchen table and collapsing into it.

"I reckon we could all use a cup about now," Mr. Walters said, motioning them all to take a seat.

Over the kitchen table and several cups of coffee, and under the pressing questions of John Walters, Shiloh and Lester shared the whole sickening story of what really went on in Camp Douglas prison camp.

"I sell horses to the army from time to time. A couple of times when I took some up to army headquarters in Alton, Colonel Mattox was there. I must say, I ain't real surprised. There was something about that fellow that didn't set right with me."

Just talking about the colonel made Shiloh's blood boil. Heat rushed up his neck to flush his face crimson. His eyes narrowed. He clinched his teeth in anger. He quickly pushed up from the table and stomped outside to walk alone in the darkness.

They spent a week with the Walters family. John and Katherine had insisted they stay and rest up before striking out on such a long and dangerous journey all the way to Tennessee.

Doc had spent the week keeping a close eye on little Andrew and nursing Mrs. Walters back to health. Kate spent her time by her mother's bedside waiting on her hand and foot. Shiloh and

Lester stayed busy helping with the many chores around the place. They cleaned out stalls, repaired the corral, and helped John Walters fix a wagon wheel.

Come to find out, Walters raised horses, some of the most beautiful animals Shiloh had ever seen. John wouldn't have nothing doing but for them pick out a horse and saddle rig apiece for their help.

"If you fellows hadn't come along when you did, I would have lost my wife and baby, no doubt about it," he told them, gulping back tears. "Three horses ain't nothing compared to what you done for me."

Doc picked out a dappled gray mare. Lester set his heart on a sorrel gelding with a white blaze face and stockings. As far as Shiloh was concerned, when he looked over the horse herd of sixty or so head, he had eyes for only one.

It was a long barreled buckskin stallion with lengthy, well-muscled legs. The magnificent animal stood a full seventeen hands high.

"That's a good choice," John Walters told him, as all four men leaned on the corral fence looking the horses over. "His name is Buck. He's a runner. He's got some Kentucky thoroughbred blood running in his veins. He likes to get frisky sometime, but as big a man as you are, you can handle him."

"John, I don't hardly know how to say what I'm about to say. It ain't like I'm asking you to spy or nothing like that, mind you. But if you hear any news about Mattox or his sergeant of the guard, the one they call the 'Bear', I'd be obliged if you'd post me a letter to Sweetwater, Tennessee. That's the closest town to my pa's place.

"I'll shore do it, Shiloh, and be glad to. I don't hold with the things that went on in that place. They ought to have to pay for what they done."

"I aim to see they do," Shiloh whispered through clenched teeth. "I aim to see they do."

They saddled and cinched their horses and led them up to the house. Katherine was sitting on the front porch in a rocking chair holding little Andrew. John disappeared into the house.

"I packed you fellows some food in those saddlebags laying there," Katherine Walters told them. "I put in the makings for coffee and a small pot. I want each of you to tie one of those blankets behind your saddle. Sometimes these nights get a little chilly."

"Thanks, Mrs. Walters," Lester said, picking up a blanket and the saddlebags. "You folks shore have been awfully nice to us."

"Now remember, ma'am," Doc told her, "don't try to do too much. I told John what to do about the stitches. A few more days and you'll be fit as a fiddle."

"I just can't thank you enough, Doctor Williams. You saved both of our lives. I'll never forget the three of you."

Lester had gone over to Johnny and Kate to say good-bye. Kate was still upset at their leaving and Johnny was wiping tears with his shirtsleeve. They both stared at the ground.

"I don't want you to go, Mr. Lester," Johnny said, trying his best not to cry.

"Now lookie here," Lester said, kneeling down. "What's all this? You're the second biggest man around here. Your pa's gonna need lots of help taking care of Kate and little Andrew and your ma. Now that's a man-size job sure enough, but I know you can handle it. Okay, partner?"

The boy swiped his eyes with the back of his hand, squared his shoulders, and offered the makings of a grin. Lester pulled upright and ruffled the boy's hair before climbing into the saddle.

John Walters hurried from the house with a holstered pistol and a gun belt wrapped around it. The shell loops were all full. He reached it out to Shiloh.

"Here," he said. "I want you to have this. It's a long way to Tennessee."

"John, there ain't no need to do that," Shiloh told him.

"This country's full of snakes," Walters said, creasing a smile. "If you know what I mean."

"I'm much obliged," Shiloh said, unrolling the gun rig and swinging it around his hips.

The two men shook hands. Shiloh swung a look at Mrs. Walters and touched a thumb and finger to his floppy old gray Confederate cavalry hat, then toed a stirrup and swung into leather.

Far down the road the three men twisted in the saddle, saw the family standing on the porch watching, and raised their hands in a final good-bye.

CHAPTER IV

May 12, 1865

The house was gone.

Shiloh blinked and couldn't believe his eyes. The house where he had been born, raised, and where his ma and pa should have been waiting on the porch, was gone. Only the rock chimney and parts of a few fire blackened logs remained.

At first sight his breath caught. Hurt, like he had never known before captured his heart, halting its beating. A lump climbed into his throat and choked him. He couldn't breath. Instinctively he knew without the words being said . . .they were dead.

He reined the buckskin to a stop. Large silver tears crept silently from his eyes and trailed slowly down his cheeks, finding refuge in month old whisker stubble. Lester and Doc glanced at the remains, then at Shiloh, and they also knew.

Shiloh raised his face to the sky. His eyes squeezed shut. His mouth opened wide. A ear-grating, raspy scream escaped his lips and echoed across the wooded hills behind where the house should have been. Horses shied. Birds fluttered from nearby trees. A cottontail rabbit scurried for cover. All who heard it could feel the hurt, injustice, and suffering of a lifetime, all released in one great, heart wrenching cry.

The graves were there, marked by a single wooden cross. Shiloh drew rein and lifted heavily from his saddle in front of the little family graveyard. He ground hitched Buck and stepped through an opening in the little picket fence.

He squatted to pull grass and weeds that had overgrown the two mounds of dirt. Sleeving away salty tears, he blinked to clear his vision and read the carved inscription on the simple cross.

ED and JOLENE WHITTINGTON
KILLED BY YANKEES
AUGUST 2, 1863.

He felt as if his heart was ripped from his chest.

They made camp that night by a little creek that meandered down out of the Appalachian Mountains on its way to the Little Tennessee river. It ran within a stone's throw of the old house. Shiloh had spent many hours as a boy in the deep hole of water, diving from the big cottonwood that leaned far out over the swimming hole.

They suppered on a roasted rabbit Lester had killed with Shiloh's pistol and wished for a cup of coffee, but settled for water from the creek. The coffee had ran out two weeks ago. They all three sat around the fire, staring quietly into the flames, listening to the night sounds. Crickets and tree frogs kept up a steady racket. A whippoorwill called and received an answer. Somewhere a night owl asked the eternal question.

"What you planning on doing now?" Lester put words to the question that had been nagging Shiloh ever since they rode in.

"I've been thinking on it," Shiloh whispered hoarsely. "Come morning we're gonna ride over to the Johnson place near

Sweetwater. I want to see what happened here. While we're there I'm gonna borrow a shovel. We're gonna do some digging.

"Mind telling me what we're digging for?" Lester asked, poking the fire with a stick.

"Don't know for shore, maybe nothing. Pa use to tell me if anything ever happened to him, look under the money tree."

"Well I'll swun," Lester drawled, "All my life I've heard that money don't grow on trees, now you're telling me you got one that does?"

"Don't know what it means," Shiloh said, " he called that big old oak over near where the barn use to sit, our money tree. I got a feeling he might have buried something there. Anyway, I'm gonna dig around some."

"What did your pa do for a living?" Doc asked.

"We farmed and raised cattle and horses. We've got six hundred'n forty acres of the best land in the Tennessee valley. Pa ran over a hundred head of good stock. We raised corn, cotton, and sorghum mostly."

"Sounds like your folks were pretty well off," Doc said.

"Looking back, I reckon we were, though we shore didn't live high on the hog. Ma used to say pa was as tight as Dick's hatband. If Pa had any money you shore wouldn't have known it."

Afterward, Shiloh spent an hour practicing drawing his pistol. It had become a regular thing every single night since John Walters gave him the rig.

"You're getting mighty swift with that rig," Lester said, as he sat watching. "Looks to me like you're practicing with a purpose in mind."

"I got a purpose," Shiloh breathed out in a raspy whisper.

The sun was high noon when they reined up in front of the Johnson place. Shiloh couldn't help expecting Elizabeth to come running out to welcome him home, her golden hair shining in the sun as he remembered.

His stomach was tied up in knots at the thought of seeing her again.

"Hello the house!" he called out, stepping down from the saddle near the familiar split rail fence.

"What you fellas want?" a gruff voice from behind them called out.

Shiloh swung a look toward the sound. Ben Johnson stood in the hallway of the nearby barn with a shotgun pointed their way. He looked a lot older than Shiloh recalled.

"Mr. Johnson, it's me, Nathan Whittington."

With a palmed hand the man shielded his eyes and leaned forward to squint through the sun's glare, peering for a long minute.

"Nath?...Is that really you? My goodness boy, I'd a never knowed you. You've growed some since I seen you." he said, lowering the gun and striding toward them with a hand out.

"How are you, Mr. Johnson?"

"Tolerable, I reckon," the man said, clasping Shiloh's hand and shaking it hard. "I figure you already been out to the old home place?"

"Yes sir. That's one reason we rode over. I wanted to see what happened?"

"Well you boys come on in the house. The wife's got on a pot of beans and a pone of cornbread and sorghum if you could make out on it."

"Shore sounds mighty good," Shiloh said. "Ben, I'd like you to shake hands with Doc Williams and Lester Posey. Lester growed up over the mountain a ways in the edge of North Carolina."

"If you boys are a riding with Nath, here, you're welcome at my table anytime," Mr. Johnson said, shaking their hands. "Are you a real doctor?"

"There's some that might argue the point, but that's about all I've ever done I guess," Doc told him as they all headed for the house.

"Shore wish you'd hang out your shingle around here,"

Mr. Johnson said. "We shore could use a doctor in this neck of the woods."

"How's the wife and Elizabeth?" Shiloh made inquiry.

"Wife's been feeling poorly," Ben said. "Don't reckon you knowed, Elizabeth married the Clymer boy from over in Sweetwater about a year ago, I guess it was. You remember him, Nath—Roy, by name. He ain't nothing but no good white trash if you ask me. His papa run the store before he died. Roy and Elizabeth run it now. Well, mostly Elizabeth does the running. Roy spends most of his time making moonshine and drinking up what he makes. Come on in boys. Wife! There'll be three more for dinner."

Shiloh's face paled and his heart plummeted. *Little old Roy Clymer? Elizabeth married that little pip-squeak?* He couldn't believe it. Mrs. Johnson hurried in with a pan of cornbread and three more plates. She was eyeing her three unexpected guests suspiciously.

"Woman," Ben said, motioning them to sit. "Take a good look at this fellow and tell me who you see?"

For a long minute she stared at Shiloh, her mind searching for an answer. Then a big smile added to the deep wrinkles already in her aging face and she reached open arms to smother him in a hug.

"Land sakes alive," she said. "If it ain't Nathan. Welcome home, boy. If you ain't a sight for sore eyes."

"Howdy do, Mrs. Johnson," Shiloh said, enjoying her hug but having a quick wish it was Elizabeth doing the hugging. Wonder if she hugged like her ma?

She loosed him from the embrace, but held him at arms length to stare at him, shaking her head in disbelief.

"Let me get a look at you, Nathan. My, you've grown a foot since I seen you last. But you always was a strapping boy. I'm real sorry about your folks. We done the burying and Ben cut their names in a cross."

"Yes ma'am, I saw. I appreciate what you done," Shiloh said, lifting out a chair and folding into it.

Lester was already spooning out a plate of beans before anyone else even got set up to the table. It had been so long since the three of them had a good meal that they forgot their manners.

"What happened to your throat, boy?" Ben asked, peering across the lip of his coffee cup. "That's a mighty nasty looking scar you're wearing around your neck."

"It's a long story, Mr. Johnson," Shiloh told him, "and not a fit one to tell around a dinner table. Tell me what happened to my folks."

"Not a whole lot to tell, son. Back in August of '63, Colonel Wilder of the Union Fourth army division swept through this part of Tennessee. They was on their way to Chattanooga just before the first big battle there.

"Some way or another, they had a list of all the local boys that was off fighting for the South. They sent squads out and murdered their families in cold blood. Then set fire to everything they owned so the boys wouldn't have nothing to come back to. Your name was on that list.

"There's been a lot of talk about how they got the list. Most think it was Abe Sawyer, though nobody can prove it. He always was one that would stop at nothing to get what he wanted.

"Seemed mighty peculiar that when the taxes come due on those places and there weren't nobody left around to pay 'em, he'd just send one of his men in and pay up the taxes and take over the place. I reckon you know he's laid claim to your place?"

"What?" Shiloh said, stopping a spoon full of beans on its way to his mouth and studying them for a long minute. "He can't do that. Pa owned our place free and clear."

"Way things are right now, I'm afraid he can, and has. Not just yours either. He's horn swoggled most everybody in this whole valley outta their land with his carpetbagger law. Judge McCormick is on his payroll, pure and simple. He's forced sheriff Potter to hire two of Abe's men as his scalawag deputies and they ain't nothing in the world but paid guns he's brought in.

"I tell you, Nath, Abe Sawyer's got this whole valley treed.

He sits up there in that big house of his and gives orders like a king or something. He never so much as shows his face, nobody's actually seen him in years, but he gets his dirty work done just the same.

"He ain't about to get my land," Shiloh whispered through clenched teeth.

White-hot anger started in his stomach. It boiled up through his neck and gave him the dry mouth. His face flushed red. His eyes squinted. Suddenly he had lost his appetite.

"Well, then you better hitch up your britches for a fight cause that's the only way you'll get it back. Anybody tries to stand up to him ends up in a world of hurt. You remember Cecil McCloud that lives up at the north end of the valley close to the river? Sawyer's been trying to get a'hold of his place. Those deputies rode out about a month ago and they beat old Cecil half to death.

"That's who I figured you fellows was when you rode up awhile ago. Sawyer's starting to work on me now, trying to get me to sell out to him. They might get it but it'll be after the fight."

Shiloh pushed back from the table and stood to his feet. He clamped his cavalry hat on his head, his mind whirling.

"Thanks, Mr. Johnson," he whispered. "We better be going."

"Thanks for the grub, Mrs. Johnson," Lester said. "It was mighty tasty." Doc nodded his agreement.

"You boys come back now," she called as they trooped toward the front door after Shiloh.

"Wonder if I could borrow a shovel?" Shiloh asked over a shoulder. "I...I need to do some work around our graveyard."

Elizabeth Clymer winced and placed a protective hand to her side. A sharp pain stabbed at her as she reached to lift a jar of peaches from a top shelf. Roy may have broken a rib this time.

The beatings were getting more frequent and came with no provocation. He was always careful to hit her where it wouldn't show. That would be bad for business. The pattern had become predictable. He slept till mid morning, left almost immediately, and stayed gone until all hours of the night, most of the time coming home falling down drunk.

On those rare occasions when he wasn't drunk, he smelled of cheap rose water used by the women at Ma Bishop's whorehouse. Elizabeth tried to pretend she was asleep, hoping it would spare her what she knew was coming. But he always woke her, pawed her with his filthy hands and breath that smelled like a hog pen, beat her, then forced himself upon her. After he was through he rolled over and went sound asleep. She cried herself to sleep.

She had known almost immediately she had made the biggest mistake of her life. But couldn't go back home and admit her error. She was afraid to tell her pa what was going on. He would kill Roy and then hang for it. She was shocked out of her self-pity by the front door opening.

"Morning Elizabeth," Mrs. Elkins said cheerfully as she pushed through the door, causing the little bell on top of the door to ring.

"Good morning," she replied, forcing a greeting that didn't reflect her true feelings. "What can I help you with this morning?"

"I need to pick up a tin of Arbuckle coffee. I ran out a few days ago. Claude gets as grouchy as an old sittin' hen if he don't have his coffee in the morning. I swear, men are all alike. Go ahead and give me a sack of dried apples too, honey. I'll bake him a pie and get him over his mad spell."

"Will there be anything else today, Mrs. Elkins?" Elizabeth asked.

"I guess not, honey. Just put that on my bill will you? Say, you remember that Whittington boy, Nathan was his name, wasn't it? You know, the one that went off to fight for the cause? Claude was riding by their old place yesterday and said he thought he saw him and a couple more fellas poking around up there. Might not have been him though, Claude said he couldn't be sure. Well, good day to you, Elizabeth."

Elizabeth stood in stunned silence, unaware of Mrs. Elkins departure.

Nathan?...Back? A rush of memories flooded her mind and brought the hint of a soft smile to her lips, the first one in a very long time. He had been her first love...no, he was the only one she ever loved.

For over two years she had dreamed of him most every night. She remembered his strong arms that had pulled her to him. His eager lips that had sought hers, and yet his kiss had been so tender, so gentle. She had relived the memory of their last good-bye a thousand times. Many nights she had drifted off into a dream world snuggled against her pillow, pretending it was Nathan.

Finally, she had forced herself to accept the belief that he was not coming back. Perhaps killed on some lonely and forgotten battlefield. She had made the conscious decision that she must forget him. She must get on with her life.

When Roy Clymer first started coming around she wasn't the least bit interested. She had known him her whole life and hadn't particularly cared for him. She had always thought of him as sort of a weakling.

He worked for his father in the large mercantile store they owned in Sweetwater, but he never seemed to have anything. His clothes were worn, his shoes run over, and his hair was always shaggy and needed cutting. He somehow managed to wait on her when she went in to pick up groceries or supplies and made his interest in her quite clear.

But he seemed to completely change. She noticed it first when he showed up at the annual box supper they had at the church. He had on a new suit, shiny boots, and his hair was even trimmed. He drove up in a brand new buggy with a black leather top, pulled by a beautiful sorrel mare.He outbid everybody for the boxed meal she had brought and they strolled off to share the fried chicken, potato salad, and cookies under the shade of a big oak tree. After that, they went riding in his new buggy most every Sunday.

Two months later they were married and moved into a pretty little white colored house at the edge of town. She didn't love Roy, but felt that in time, she could grow into it. From the very start, their love life left her frustrated and unfulfilled. Without feeling, it quickly became a matter of fulfilling her duty as a wife.

At least her future would be secure, she reasoned. Roy always seemed to have money and bought her new things regularly, even though he no longer worked for his father in the store. Then his father dropped dead in the store one day. Less than three months later he lost his mother.

They had been married less that six months when the drinking started.

At first she blamed it on the loss of his parents and made excuses for him. He began drinking heavier and coming in later and later. She well remembered the first night she smelled the perfume when he came home. She confronted him with it and an argument quickly escalated into a shouting match and ended with him punching her in the stomach. After that the beatings got. . .

"Mrs. Clymer, are you okay?"

"What...oh...I'm sorry. I didn't hear you come in," she said, glancing up through a tear-wet gaze.

Mr. Streeter stood only a few feet away staring with a concerned look.

"Excuse me for saying so, Mrs. Clymer, but you had a terrible scared look on your face just now. Is something wrong?"

"No, nothing. How can I help you today?" she hurried to ask.

"I'm needing a half dozen sacks of oats to tide me over till the crop comes in. I backed my wagon up to the loading dock."

"I...well...I don't know. Roy isn't here just now and I don't have any way to load them."

"Don't you worry none about that, ma'am. If you'll fix up the bill I'll do the loading."

After Mr. Streeter left Elizabeth couldn't hold it in any longer. She felt jagged inside. Long pent up emotions surged through her and erupted in great sobs that shook her small frame. She buried her face in her hands and collapsed into a cane bottom chair.

Shiloh's booted foot forced the shovel point deep into the soft, rich ground. His arm muscles bulged. Sweat poured from his face and shirtless back. Again and again, he lifted dirt from the four foot deep hole to pile it on the growing mound around the hole. They had begun their digging at the base of the tree. After completing a three foot wide path around it and finding nothing but tree roots, they expanded their search in an ever widening circle.

If only he could remember exactly what his pa had said. It had only been talked of a couple of times that he could recall. The last time was just before he rode off to join the army. They had been forking hay down from the hayloft in the barn and had stopped to pump up a drink of water.

"Son, that big old oak over there, that's our money tree," he remembered his pa saying. "If anything ever happens to me, look under it."

He wished now he'd asked his pa what he meant. Maybe that's not what he meant at all, Shiloh began to consider. They had been digging steady for most of a half day, and the only thing they had to show for their effort was a bunch of blisters.

"I reckon we're wasting our time," he finally gasped. Disappointment clouded his face. He chucked the shovel out of the hole and climbed out behind it. He sat down and hung his head dejectedly.

"Let me take another turn," Lester said, his expression saying he wasn't so sure. Scooping up the shovel, he jumped into the hole.

Shiloh lifted his head and watched his friend working the shovel with his one hand. Doc was lying back on the soft grass, completely exhausted from his part in the digging.

"It's no use, Lester," Shiloh said. "There's nothing there."

He had no more than turned loose of the words when the unmistakable grating of metal on metal reached his ears. He was instantly on his feet and jumped into the hole.

"There's something there," Lester shouted excitedly. "Look! Look! Right there."

Shiloh snatched the shovel from Lester's hand and started scooping dirt away from the top of a metal chest. Doc landed beside him. All three fell to their knees, scratching and clawing at the dirt like three dogs digging for the same bone.

"We found it!" Lester shouted. "Can you believe it? We found it!"

The metal strongbox was now clearly visible. It was large, looking to be about eighteen inches by eighteen inches by twenty-four inches long. Shiloh grasped one of the handles on either end and tugged it free. A lock hasp was rusted closed but contained no lock. Using the shovel point he broke the hasp loose. It took a few tries to pry the lid open. The rusty hinges complained and resisted, but finally gave way. Shiloh slowly raised the lid.

"Holy smokes!" Lester exclaimed as he stared into the box.

Shiloh's heart skipped a few beats and a huge lump climbed its way into his throat. The chest was three-quarters full of shiny twenty dollar gold double eagles. On top of the fortune in gold lay a leather money belt and a folded paper.

Reaching a thumb and finger Shiloh picked up the paper.

With shaking hands he slowly unfolded it. Through tear washed eyes he read his pa's scribbled printing.

Dear son,

The fact that you're reading this means your mother and i have both gone on to meet our reward and you have returned safe from the war.

Since the day you were born, all we ever wanted was for you to be happy. Over the years we saved this for you. This is not the measure of our love, no chest would be large enough to hold all that. We both love you son.

Your pa and ma

For a few long minutes he stared down at the fortune lying there before him. What he saw wasn't the shiny double eagles, but a lifetime of skimping and saving, of making do with less for themselves, so they could leave something for him.

Swiping tears from his eyes with the back of his hand, he unfolded the other legal looking paper. It was a warranty deed for the 64 acres. He folded it back and shot a quick glance at Lester and Doc. They were still staring, bug-eyed, at the chest full of money.

Lester reached his hand timidly, scooping it full, and letting the shiny gold coins escape through spread fingers and fall back to join their companions.

"Whooew," he exclaimed. "Now that's a bunch of money. How much you figure's there?"

"Enough that we'll never have to go without from now on," Shiloh rasped out.

Lifting the money belt, Shiloh unsnapped one of the compartment flaps. Inside he found folded bills, both Confederate and Federal. Examining each of the six little pouches, he found them filled with the same thing.

For a long time none of them moved. They sat in the

hole around the strongbox, staring unbelieving at the fortune before them.

Again, that night they camped by the swimming hole. They swam and splashed happily in the cool water like three schoolboys until sundown. After washing their ragged clothes as best they could Doc used his surgical scissors to trim both Shiloh's and Lester's hair and beards. Shiloh returned the favor. Sitting around their campfire on the creek bank, they talked far into the night, trying to ignore their growling stomachs.

"I promise you fellows," Shiloh told them. "This is the last night you'll go to bed hungry."

CHAPTER V

Sweetwater, Tennessee was a sleepy little town. What few people were out and about moved lazily among the three dozen or so false-fronted clapboard buildings that lined the single dusty street, as if they had no place in particular to go and were taking their own sweet time getting there. But this was only Thursday. Saturday would be a different matter. Everybody came to town on Saturday.

A wooden bridge spanned Sweetwater creek that trailed along the valley and marked the start of town. A square whitewashed church with a tall steeple sat on a sloping hillside at the edge of town and served as a school during the week. Shiloh recalled his years there. It must have been mid morning recess because twenty of more children were running and playing in the churchyard.

A few of the older boys stopped and gawked as the three riders crossed the bridge. The horse's shod hooves make loud clopping sounds on the heavy planks.

"This place hadn't changed a bit," Shiloh whispered hoarsely.

"Man-oh-man," Lester exclaimed, lifting a finger to point. "Who lives in that big house up there on top of the hill?"

"That's Abe Sawyer's place," Shiloh said, anger biting into his voice. "He's the one that's trying to steal my land."

"Is he the one that never leaves his house?" doc asked.

"Yeah," Shiloh told them. "He's real weird. Kind of a hermit I reckon you'd call him. I was raised here and I've never actually laid eyes on him."

They reined up in front of the livery stable and swung down. Old man Beam limped out to take charge of their mounts. He glanced up from under bushy gray eyebrows and swept them with an appraising glance, looked away, then did a double take when his eyes fell on Shiloh, a hint of recognition dawning in his eyes.

"Ain't you...? Ain't you the Whittington boy?" he asked hesitantly.

"Yes sir, Mr. Beam," Shiloh said, sticking out a hand. "Nathan."

"Why shore it is. You're the spitting image of your pa. It's been a long spell, boy."

"More'n four years," Shiloh said, loosening the cinch straps on his buckskin. "Mr. Beam, I'd like you to meet my friends. This is Doctor Williams, and the ugly one is Lester Posey."

They shook hands all around while pulling saddles from their horses and swinging them on the top board of a nearby stall.

"We'll need our horses stalled and grain fed," Shiloh told the old fellow, fishing a shiny double eagle from his pocket and flipping it to the holster.

"I ain't got no change," the man said, snatching it deftly out of the air.

"None's needed, we may be staying awhile."

"Hope so, we shore could use a doctor in these parts since old doctor Adams kicked the bucket a couple of years back."

"We'll be over at the boarding house," Shiloh said, turning on his heels.

The white, two story, box-like house was surrounded by a white picket fence. The gate squeaked in protest as they made their way through and up the steps to a wide porch. A porch swing hung on either end. It was a friendly looking place. A heavyset woman with an apron wrapped around her ample middle and even larger derriere looked up from sweeping and flashed a friendly smile as they pushed through the front door.

"You gents looking for a room?" she asked cheerfully, then, not waiting for an answer, "The price is a dollar a day each or five dollars by the week. There's two meals a day. Breakfast is at six sharp. If you're late you do without. Supper is anytime between five and seven. I change the sheets once a week. I don't allow no loud cussing nor fighting. How many rooms will you be needing?"

"We'll want three," Shiloh told her. "I'm called Shiloh. This is Doc Williams and that's Lester Posey. If the food's good we're liable to be staying awhile. If it ain't, we'll be leaving at the end of the week." He laid a double eagle on the counter.

"Then you'll be staying a spell. I like a fellow that speaks his mind," she said, "I'm Kate Solesbee. You boys will be at the top of the stairs, first three rooms on the left overlooking the street. I save my best rooms for my long term customers."

"Thank you ma'am," Lester said, touching a finger to his floppy hat. "You say supper is at five?"

"Piping hot and licking good," she said, a big smile crinkling the corners of her mouth. "You gonna be setting up a practice here in Sweetwater, Doctor?"

"Yes ma'am," Doc said. "Least wise I'm thinking on it."

"Well now, that's the best news I've heard in a coon's age," the friendly woman said. "We sure need a good doctor around here. Are you any good?"

"He's most likely the best sawbones that ever doctored man or beast," Lester assured her, patting Doc on the shoulder.

"I do my best," Doc Williams said, embarrassed.

"Where could we find a bath?" Shiloh made inquiry. "We could stand some freshening up, I reckon."

"Up the street on the right," Kate told them. "Bath & Barber, it's called. Dudley Harvey owns the place. He'll have you gents all spruced up in nothing flat."

"What say we mosey up that way?" Shiloh asked. "We'll be needing some clothes. Let's go by the Mercantile store on the way."

"I don't know if I can part with these," Lester said. "We've kinda grown attached to each other."

"Yeah," Doc chimed in, "but your hide is peeking through in some mighty embarrassing places."

"We'll shore be back in time for supper," Lester called over his shoulder as they pushed out the door.

Shiloh was shaking like a leaf in a whirlwind as they stepped up onto the boardwalk in front of Clymer's Mercantile & Feed. Would Elizabeth be there? Would she even remember him? How should he act? After all, she was a married woman now. He pushed the door open. A bell sounded. She looked up from a ledger where she sat at a small desk. He drew a sharp inhale of breath.

She wore a yellow checked gingham, ankle length dress. Her long, blonde hair was pulled back and tied with a matching yellow ribbon that trailed near as long as the golden curls of hair. Tiny ringlets strayed loosely and framed the same perky face he remembered. Her blue eyes rounded when she recognized him.

"Nathan? Is that you?" she gasped, an unbelieving look on her pretty face.

Her heart beat rapidly. For a long moment she hesitated, then shot to her feet and flew across the floor into his arms. They held each other tightly for a lingering space of time.

"Thank God you're home safe," she whispered through sobs of happiness. Salty tears wet her cheeks.

Finally, they released each other and he held her at arms length to gaze at her closely.

"You're even more beautiful than when I left," he rasped the words out, embarrassed at the sound. "I hope you can excuse my voice, I...I hurt my throat."

"I'm sorry," she said, her voice sounding concerned. "But you're home. That's the only thing that matters."

"I rode over to your folk's house. They told me you are..."

"Yes," she interrupted, not wanting to hear him say the word. She dropped her face to gaze at the floor and blinked away eyelids full of tears. "I didn't think."

"I understand," he told her, releasing his hands from her shoulders. "How is Roy?"

"He's...well, he's drinking an awful lot lately."

"Oh, I see," Shiloh whispered, thinking he better change the subject.

"Me and my friends need some new duds. Think you can fix us up?"

"I'll bet I can," she said, her voice resuming the happy sound he remembered from so long ago. "Right this way."

Elizabeth stood, staring out the window after them. She felt giddy and lightheaded. She watched Nathan as he strode along beside his friends. He was tall, taller than she remembered, well over six feet, and filled out too. His wide shoulder muscles bulged even under the ragged shirt he wore. She had felt his arm muscles when he held her. He walked erect and proud, a man sure of himself. She liked that. The low slung gun on his right hip looked natural, as if it were born there.

A shiver ran through her and her face flushed with a thought. What if? No! It was too late for what ifs. She was a married woman. She shouldn't be thinking those kinds of thoughts. Besides, he most likely wouldn't be interested in her now anyway.

They all three felt, and looked like new men when they stepped from the Bath & Barber. Doc had chosen a black, three piece broadcloth suit. With his new black boots and his black

Stetson, he looked more like a banker than a doctor. Lester wore brown, high-heeled boots, dark brown pants, and a chocolate brown shirt, with his armless sleeve pinned up elbow length.

At the insistence of Elizabeth, Shiloh had settled on black, high-heeled boots that made him feel three inches taller than his six foot two inches. Black pants, and a beautiful blue shirt, with a light blue neckerchief, done a whole lot for his confidence. Even his gun rig seemed to match his new getup perfectly.

"If you fellows don't look all gussied up," Lester kidded. "Feels like we're on our way to a church social or something."

"You clean up pretty good yourself," Shiloh told his friend as they headed back toward the boarding house.

They passed a saloon. The sound of an off-key piano drifted through the batwing doors. Shiloh saw Doc cut an eye in that direction.

Shiloh slanted a grin.

"I reckon we've got time to wet our whistle if you fellows got a hankering," he said, reading Doc's thinking as if he had said the words out loud.

"Don't mind if I do," Doc said, breaking a grin.

"Hate to even think how long it's been," Lester chimed in, pushing through the swinging doors. Doc and Shiloh followed.

The musty stench of stale whiskey and cigarette smoke greeted them and hung like a cloud in the place. It burned Shiloh's nose as they bellied up to the bar.

His glance circled the room and revealed four men playing poker at a table, two other gents nursed drinks at another, and some fellow was draped all over a pretty bar girl at a table near the back. A short, bald headed piano player offered them only a quick glance then redirected his eyes back to his playing.

It was the two tough looking jaspers standing at the end of the bar that warranted a longer look. One was a big burley fellow with wide shoulders and a neck near as big around as his head.

He looked as if he could fight a grizzly bear bare handed and not even break a sweat. The other was a big man, lean and bony. He wore a black flat brimmed hat that was pulled low and hid most of his face in its shadow as he steadied his drink. Those two were trouble waiting to happen if Shiloh had ever seen it.

"What'll you boys have?" the barkeep asked, wiping the top of the bar in front of them.

"Give me a double from the bottle you most likely keep under the counter," Doc said.

"Yeah," Lester agreed. "Make it two."

"Nothing for me," Shiloh whispered, dropping two coins on the bar and flicking another glance at the two fellows at the end of the bar.

The burley fellow had a stare fixed on Shiloh. He said something low to his companion that Shiloh couldn't hear. Both men wore deputy's badges pinned to their shirts. The man in the black hat slowly lifted his face...and Shiloh saw the face of death.

He was a tall man, rangy and long boned, a hard man, his face weathered down to its elements. Skin stretched tight over his protruding cheekbones. A prominent Adams apple, jutting chin and a thin slash of mouth gave way to a hooked nose. But the eyes, pale and cold as an outhouse in the middle of winter, were what captured Shiloh's attention. They locked on Shiloh.

"Come on, Shiloh," Lester said, "Have one with us."

"No thanks. I never had a taste for it," he told his friend, shifting his eyes from the thin fellow.

"Hey, Buford," a slurred voice from the fellow with the bargirl called out. "Bring us another bottle over here and make it snappy."

"Just keep your shirt on, Roy," the barkeep told him. "Can't you see I'm busy right now?"

Shiloh cut his eyes to the back table and examined the fellow closer. Sure enough. It was Roy Clymer, Elizabeth's husband. She was working the store all by herself while he was boozing it up with some hussy in a bar.

How could the man do that? He had the most beautiful girl in the valley as his wife and...well, it was none of his affair. He made himself a promise not to get involved.

"You boys enjoy your drink and I'll meet you back at the boarding house," he told Lester, then, lowering his voice whispered. "Watch yourself."

He turned and strode from the saloon without looking back. Those two tough looking fellows had to be the deputies Ben Johnson had told him about. The ones that Abe Sawyer had brought in to do his dirty work. They sure looked up to the job; he had never seen a scarier looking hombre than the skinny one.

The Monroe County courthouse was a two-story masonry building that sat in the very center of town. The second floor served as the county jail. Shiloh climbed the stone steps and stepped through the tall double doors into a wide hallway. He found the county clerk's office and pushed inside. A short, red faced fellow looked up from a ledger and eyed him for a long moment.

"Well if it ain't Nathan Whittington," he said, a smile wrinkling his features.

"Rudy?" Shiloh asked, recognition coming to him. "Rudy Stiles? Well I'll be a monkey's uncle. I ain't seen you since we was in school together. I thought you and your folks moved to Nashville."

"We did. They passed on a couple years back. I never did like it in the big city so I up and moved back to the valley."

"Don't tell me you're the county clerk now?"

"Yep. I worked in the land office in Nashville for a few years. When I moved back here, folks said since I had experience in that sort of thing, I'd make a good county clerk, so here I am. Hey, it's good to see you made it back home safe. A lot of our friends didn't. I'm real sorry about your folks."

"Yeah," Shiloh said, "that's why I'm here. What's all this about Abe Sawyer trying to take my land?"

The happy smile on Rudy's face suddenly dissolved. His face turned a bright red. His eyes rounded and shifted nervously toward the door. From the looks of him, you would have thought he was climbing the steps to a gallows for his own hanging.

"You—you don't understand how it is," he stammered, great drops of sweat popping out on his forehead.

"You're almighty right about that, Rudy," Shiloh whispered. "So why don't you explain it to me."

"It's none of my doing, Nath, honest. The judge and—"

"The judge? That would be Isaac McCormick?" Shiloh asked. "Who did you mean when you said, and?"

"What?" Rudy asked, looking like he wished he were someplace else.

"You *said,* and I just asked who you were talking about?"

"I can't tell you that, Nath. They'd kill me."

"Rudy. Now you listen and listen close. I rode off to fight for a cause I believed in. I've seen more death than I even want to think about. I just spent near two years in a hellhole prisoner of war camp. I had to kill seven of my own fellow prisoners, just to survive. I was hanged and left for dead. I come home to find out my folks were murdered because some no good traitor gave the blue bellies a list of us boys that was off fighting for the south. Our farm was burned to the ground and now I hear Abe Sawyer's figured out a way to take what's mine?

"Now, Rudy, we've known each other a long time. I reckon you know I ain't gonna let that happen. You better start talking to me and it better be right sudden 'cause I'm about to run out of patience."

"Nath... I'm sorry. There's this law they're using to take land away from people. It says if the taxes aren't paid for three years running the sheriff offers the land for public sale on the courthouse steps to anyone that will pay up the back taxes.

"They just forget to tell anybody when it's gonna be sold and Abe or one his men shows up and pays the taxes. The judge rules the sale legal and orders me to issue a quit claim deed."

"Can they really do that?" Shiloh's voice rang ragged with outrage. "Is that the law?"

"Well," Rudy said, "it's the law all right, at least that's part of it. The rest of the law says the original owner of the property has another five years to catch up the taxes. If he does, the property reverts back to him and the quit claim deed becomes null and void."

"So that means if I pay up the taxes on our place, then Sawyer no longer has a claim to it?" Shiloh asked.

"That's what it means," Rudy told him.

"How much taxes do I owe on my place?"

"Just a minute. Let me look it up."

The clerk pulled down a thick book and flipped through the pages, then ran his finger down a long column of figures. He stared for a long space of time at the figures, flipped back a few pages, then scratched his head in puzzlement.

"There's something bad wrong here," he said. "According to this, the only back taxes owed are for 1863 and 64. This year's taxes aren't even due yet. This land shouldn't have been sold or a quit claim deed issued on your place for another year. All you owe is for the two years. That comes to eighty two dollars."

"How could that happen?" Shiloh asked.

"I sure didn't issue a seizure notice. The only other person that could have is a clerk that works part time for me. He's not in today, but you can bet your boots I'm gonna be asking some hard questions when he comes in tomorrow."

Shiloh counted out the eighty two dollars and laid it on the counter.

"I'll fill out the paperwork and give you a receipt. You'll have to take it to the judge and get him to issue a ruling canceling the quit claim deed on your place. Do you have your original deed signing it over to you?"

"Yeah," Shiloh said, pulling the document from his pocket.

"Pa signed it and put it in a safe place in case something happened to him. It's a good thing he did."

"Just take these papers and your deed down the hall to the judge and see if he'll sign them. If he won't, your only chance then is going to the Attorney General in Nashville. I'm real sorry, Nath. I'll most likely get in big trouble for helping you, but it just ain't right what they're trying to do."

"Thanks, Rudy. I appreciate what you done. I won't be forgetting it. Just in case, what's the Attorney General's name?"

"Miles Stapelton," Rudy told him. "His office is in the state capitol building. He's a good man."

Shiloh's boot heels made tromping sounds on the bare wood floor as he strode down the hallway. At the door to the judge's office he slowed only long enough to turn the knob before pushing through. The little brass nameplate sitting on the desk read, *Isaac McCormick County Judge.*

"Who are you?" the pudgy faced fellow with tiny spectacles perched out on the end of his nose demanded. "It's customary to knock before entering one's office unannounced."

The judge sat behind a large desk smoking a fat cigar. He looked to be an average sized fellow, maybe leaning a little toward the heavy side, maybe hadn't missed any meals in a long spell. His gray hair was thinning on top and showed a shiny bald spot. He wore a black, three piece broadcloth suit.

"I'm Nathan Whittington," Shiloh forced the words out hoarsely. "Son of Ed and Jolene Whittington. The Yankees murdered my folks and burned their house and barn to the ground. I want to know why you issued a quit claim deed to Abe Sawyer for the six hundred and forty acres they left to me free and clear?"

"I'm not in the habit of answering questions when someone storms into my office unannounced," the judge said, anger coloring his face. He jerked the cigar from his mouth and shot to his feet.

"I'm not in the habit of asking a question more'n once either,"

Shiloh spat out the words, leaning far over the desk, anger boiling red in his eyes. He fixed a stare and aimed a thick finger at the judge. "Now, either I get some answers right sudden, or I'll take a ride up to the capitol and see my friend, Miles Stapelton, the Attorney General. He's liable to be right interested in what's going on around here."

For a long moment their eyes locked on each other. The judge licked his lips. His eyes began to blink rapidly.

"I could have you arrested," he blurted out, suddenly sounding unsure of his position.

"I reckon you could, but then Miles might be asking some mighty tough questions about the why of it. Now, I'm gonna break my own rule and ask you just once more." Shiloh said drawing his lips back over clenched teeth. "I'm waiting for an answer."

"I suppose if I issued Mr. Sawyer a quit claim deed on your place it was because it was sold for nonpayment of taxes."

"The taxes were only past due for two years, and that's because my parents were murdered and I was off fighting a war. The law says taxes have to be late three consecutive years before it's sold," Shiloh told him. "Look at the papers yourself and you'll see. It's right there."

A frightened, almost frantic look occupied the judge's face as he picked up the papers and studied them closely.

"Uh-umph! well, there does seem to be some kind of mistake here," the man said. "I'll look into it."

"No, sir," Shiloh said, pushing his advantage. "That ain't good enough. I want an affidavit, signed by you, voiding the bogus quit claim you gave Abe Sawyer on my property and I want it right now."

Shiloh stalked out the door, leaving behind a badly shaken judge fumbling out an apology. Shiloh's only answer was the loud slamming of the door to the judge's office as he left. He stuffed the signed affidavit in his pocket and headed toward the boarding house. His eyes drifted across the street to Clymer's Mercantile and fought the tugging urge to go by to see Elizabeth.

Doc and Lester were sitting on the porch of the boarding house in one of the porch swings, sipping coffee and looking mighty contented.

"Figured you boys would still be over at the watering hole," Shiloh said as he climbed the steps.

"Those two deputies at the end of the bar started asking a lot of questions after you left," Lester told him. "They wanted to know who you was and what we were doing in Sweetwater. They made it clear we weren't exactly welcome around here."

"They might just as well get use to the idea," Shiloh said. "This is our home and we ain't going nowhere."

"I got a feeling we're gonna have a run-in with those two before it's all settled," Lester said, sipping his coffee.

"I don't want trouble unless it's brought to me," Shiloh said, sitting down on the edge of the porch and leaning his back against a post, "but I ain't never left a place till I was ready to go."

"That's kind of my feeling about it too," Lester told him. "Think I'll mosey down to the store in the morning. I sorta took a liking to a sawed off scattergun I saw when we was in there awhile ago. Might come in right handy before this is all said and done."

"I don't want you and Doc buying in to my troubles, I can stomp my own snakes."

"It's kind of like you said a minute ago," Doc chimed in. "This is our home now, too. If it's a fight they're looking for, I'll side you boys."

"You boys gonna sit there gabbing all night?" Kate asked in a loud voice from just inside the screen door. "Supper's hot and set."

"Now that's sweet music to my ears," Lester said, pulling himself to his feet. "I ain't one to keep supper waiting."

The big dining room table would seat eight. Bowls of

steaming food sat on the red and white checkered oilcloth covering. Two other men were already filling their plates and glanced up briefly when Lester, Doc, and Shiloh strode in and scraped out chairs.

Over supper they learned one of them was a drummer from Chattanooga named Oscar Hogan that came through once a month to call on Clymer's store. The other was a young lawyer named Clayton Moore that had just arrived that day.

"You figuring on setting up shop here in Sweetwater?" Shiloh asked the young fellow that looked to be about his own age.

"Yes sir. I've been working as an intern for Adams & Barker law firm in Nashville for the past two years since I got my license. I've decided it's time to set up my own practice. This seems like a nice place to live."

"Doc here is thinking on hanging out his shingle in Sweetwater, too," Lester said between mouthfuls.

"Town's getting downright civilized," Kate said in her boisterous voice, sweeping in and setting a pot of coffee on the table. "What with doctors and lawyers and the likes coming in."

"Are there any vacant buildings in town one might rent?" the young attorney asked.

Kate stopped and stared at the ceiling a moment, considering the question, before answering.

"You might talk to Sid Morrison, the undertaker," she told him. "He's got a small building next door to his place. He might be willing to rent it out."

"Thanks, Mrs. Solesbee," the young lawyer said. "I'll talk to him first thing in the morning. Have you found a location yet, Doctor Williams?"

"Haven't had time to look," Doc said, "we just rode in today, too. I was thinking I might build a place."

After supper, the drummer left, saying he was gonna have himself a drink or two before he turned in. The rest of them lingered around the table over another cup of coffee and visited for an hour or so. Shiloh decided he liked the young lawyer.

"I don't know about you fellows," Doc told them, pulling stiffly to his feet, "but my old bones are plumb tuckered out. I'm gonna see what a real bed feels like. It's been so long I forgot."

"Think I'll see if that pretty little gal over at the saloon is still occupied," Lester said. "She was giving me some mighty inviting looks while that fellow was pawing her. Want to come along?" he asked Shiloh.

"No thanks. I'm gonna get me a breath of fresh air then hit the sack myself."

"Shore was a mighty fine meal, Miss Kate," Lester hollered back to the kitchen.

"Buttering me up won't get you nothing extra, young fellow," she shouted back.

They all chuckled at Miss Kate's outward brashness because it was apparent she wasn't really like that at all. Shiloh helped himself to another cup of coffee, then strolled out to the porch and leaned against a post. He leisurely sipped the steaming liquid and watched Lester disappear into the darkness on his way toward the saloon.

A vague uneasiness tugged at him. There was an ugly undercurrent bubbling just under the surface of the outwardly peaceful little town. He had a feeling it wouldn't take much for it to erupt into violence.

His actions earlier at the Judge's office in forcing the return of his land most likely wouldn't be taken lightly by Abe Sawyer. It was crystal clear the two deputies were itching for a fight.

Wonder where the sheriff stands in all this? Best I remember, Sheriff Potter always seemed like a good man—but even good men sometimes go bad. Shiloh decided he'd stop by and have a talk with the sheriff the next day.

When he had seen Roy Clymer in the saloon that afternoon

with the bargirl, it troubled Shiloh's mind. What kind of man would slop around in a saloon while his wife worked her head off earning the money he was drinking up?

What would drive a fellow to even look cross-eyed at a bargirl when he had the most beautiful girl in the whole valley waiting for him at home?Casually, Shiloh strolled down the steps and along the path toward the street, not really headed anywhere, but just feeling a need to walk.

His mind sorted through all the events that had happened since he had returned home and considered the options of what to do next. It still amazed him at the large amount of money his folks had left him. The chest of money was safe for now, hidden in a tiny cave he had discovered as a boy and which no one else knew about. He had no idea how much the chestcontained. After counting out five hundred dollars apiece from the gold coins for Doc, Lester, and himself, he could hardly tell the amount had gone down. Even though Shiloh wanted to rebuild the house and barn the Yankees had burned he wasn't really sure he wanted to be a farmer. He liked cattle and

horses. Maybe he could start building a small herd. But somehow the things that should be exciting to him didn't seem to matter all that much. There was something else gnawing at him deep inside, something that was more important than the money, or rebuilding the old home place, or starting aherd of horses or cattle.

Unconsciously his hand went to his throat, threaded under the heavy neckerchief and trailed along the ugly scar that ringed his neck. Samuel Mattox! The thought hit him like a runaway wagon. Suddenly, Shiloh knew what he had to do; nothing else mattered until that part of his life was settled. Somehow, I've got to find the colonel and set things right. No matter where I got to go, no matter how long it takes. Until then, I can't get on with my life.

The gentle sound of gurgling water tugged his mind back to the present. He blinked his eyes and realized that without even knowing it, he had strolled to the edge of town. He stood on the grassy creekbank under the big old willow tree where he and Elizabeth had slipped away from church and met a few times before he went away. They called it their special place.

A cool evening breeze whispered through long, spindly willow limbs and lifted them to wave at the night as they emitted a low, whistling sound. Somehow it was appropriate that he was here on this particular night. The mournful sound reflected his own feelings.

The early summer night sky was alive with a million twinkling stars peeking through a canopy of inky blackness. Light from a thin slice of a quarter-moon filtered through the willow limbs and made dancing shadows on the soft grass under his feet.

His gaze lifted to the shining orb. His mind drifted back to all those nights on the battlefield and in the prison camp when he had stared up at that same moon, wishing he was back home with his ma and pa and Elizabeth.

"It's beautiful isn't it?"

The soft words from a familiar voice came from behind him.

Startled, he whirled. Elizabeth was there! Moonlight touched her hair and set it ablaze, framing her face with a golden hue. She wore a soft blue, ankle length dress, cut low in the front. A white, crocheted shawl draped across her shoulders, but failed to hide the beginning of her womanly breasts that peeked timidly above the neckline. His gaze landed there and lingered.

A sudden hitch in his breathing took his breath away. He tore his eyes away and tugged his thoughts back from where they didn't belong. His face flushed with questions his mind had been asking. His eyes drank in her breathtaking beauty. She was a picture for a man to hold in his mind.

"I'm sorry," she said, brushing a windblown lock of hair from her face with a finger. "I didn't mean to startle you."

"Oh, no," he stammered. "I guess I was just lost in my memories."

"I understand. I have nice memories of this place too. I come here often."

"It's a peaceful place, our special place. Remember?"

"I remember," he whispered.

Her sparkling eyes searched his face as she spoke softly. "When I'm here I feel...I guess I feel like that teenage girl again. So young and innocent and excited and safe."

"Lots of nights on the battlefield when the guns were going off all around me, I would look up at the moon and think of this place," he told her.

"Did you ever think of me?" she asked.

"Most every night, I reckon."

"What did you think?"

He turned his head to look down at her standing there beside him. Her face lifted. Her gaze connected with his. The moonlight reflected across the rippling water and bathed her features with shimmering points of light. His heart raced. He swallowed a huge lump in his throat and captured a deep breath of air.

"I would remember the times we were here together—how much I missed you—how beautiful you are. Sometimes I could close my eyes and remember how your lips tasted when we kissed. I would make plans how, when I got back home, we—"

"Nathan, I'm so sorry I didn't wait. You were gone so long and I never heard a word from you for over two years. I didn't know if you were alive or if you had been killed. If only I'd known you would come back someday, I would have waited, no matter how long it took. I wanted to."

"It wasn't your fault," Shiloh whispered. "I was thinking, not long ago, how I wished I'd told my folks how much I loved them more often. Looking back, I wish now I'd made it clearer how I felt about you before I left. I reckon we would all do some things different if we got the chance. But wishing it don't make it so. The way I see it, yesterday is gone and we can't go back and do it different. We can't live tomorrow till it gets here. So all we have is today."

Words weren't working; He knew he was babbling, but he dared not say what his heart was screaming out to be said. Shiloh deliberately looked away, shifting his gaze to the fireflies that flitted and sparkled among the trees.

"Nathan..." Elizabeth whispered, lifting her face closer, her voice breathy and low. He searched her questioning eyes and had no answer. "Would you kiss me?"

Shiloh's heart leaped into his suddenly scratchy-dry throat. Must be the wind making my throat so dry, he thought. His strong arm crept slowly around her shoulders. His other hand came to rest on her waist.

His mouth brushed hers. Deliberately light, excruciatingly slow. Her lips were soft. The kiss was tender and sweet and tasted like a fresh, ripe strawberry. His eyes were closed, but he felt a tremor surge through her body. A sound escaped her lips, half protest, half plea, followed by a deep, throaty moan that shook his soul. Their lips tore apart, and their eyes searched the other's gaze for a long moment.

Golden strands of windblown hair touched her flushed cheeks. He saw a pleading look in her blue eyes. But there was also something else reflected there, a look of sadness, a sadness he was determined to soothe.

Her arms encircled his neck and pulled his mouth to hers with an urgency that would not be denied. Warm and welcoming lips opened. Her breath came in short gasps. Her mouth ground into his with a long stifled, starving hunger.

A ribbon of desire coiled tightly in the pit of his stomach. It was too late. He couldn't walk away now.

CHAPTER VI

The morning sun crept silently through the window, filtered through lacy curtains, and warmed Shiloh's face. His eyes flicked open. Memories of the night before flooded his mind with a strange mixture of both satisfaction and guilt; the former feeling definitely more enjoyable than the latter.

Throwing back the sheet, he swung his feet to the floor and pushed upright.

Lifting long arms high over his head, he stretched, then pulled his fingers through his hair before strolling over to gaze out the window.

The sun was already arching above the rooftops of the houses across the street. He had missed breakfast. Pouring water from the blue speckled pitcher into the matching pan, he washed up, quickly shaved and dressed and headed downstairs.

"You're way too late for breakfast," Kate scolded loudly, sweeping the dining room with a straw broom, "but the coffee's still hot."

"Thanks," Shiloh said, trying unsuccessfully to clear the hoarseness from his throat. "That would go good."

Miss Kate pushed through the door onto the porch, wiping her hands on an apron tied around her ample waist.

"Doc's done gone," she told him loudly. "Said he was gonna look around for a place to put his office. Lester didn't come in at all last night. You didn't beat him much."

"What'd you do?" Shiloh asked, sipping his coffee. "Wait up for us?"

"Ain't nothing but trouble a man can get into after midnight in this town," she said plainly. She didn't know how right she was.

"Reckon I better go see if I can find Lester," he said, draining his cup and tying the holster cord to his right leg.

He pushed out the front door and started down the steps. Lester was coming down the boardwalk. Shiloh sat down on the edge of the porch.

"Boy, you look like you've been rode hard and put away wet," he told his friend as Lester stumbled up the path.

"I think I'm in love," Lester said, dropping down on the porch and stretching out on his back.

"If love makes you look like you look, seems to me you'd be better off without it."

"Lord, lord, partner. You just don't know. I've been to heaven and back a dozen times since I seen you. That Maybelle is a *one of a kind* sort of woman."

"Yeah, well I'm right proud for you, but you better get some rest before you go see her again. I doubt you could make it through another night the way you look. Besides, you're too late for breakfast."

"A man does not live by food alone, the traveling preacher used to say," Lester said, stretching his arms out above his head.

"Now I know you're in bad shape," Shiloh told him, "starting to quote a preacher. You see anything of Doc?"

"No," Lester said, sitting upright. "Ain't you seen him this morning?"

"He was already gone when I got up. Kate said he was

going to look for a place to put his doctor's office. Think I'll look around a bit."

"Want me to come with you?"

"No. You better get some sleep. We'll see you after awhile."

He found the Doc in front of the undertaker's office talking to a beanpole of a fellow. Shiloh assumed it was the undertaker since he sorely resembled an undertaker. The man was tall and thin, no bigger around than a fence post. He wore black pants and a black, long tailed coat. His face was chalky white.

"Shiloh, this is Mr. Morrison. He's the undertaker hereabouts. I just rented the little building next door for my office."

"I thought the young lawyer was looking at it," Shiloh said.

"He come and looked at it," the undertaker said in a preachy voice. "He decided it was too small for what he wanted."

"That's good Doc," Shiloh said. "When are you gonna move in and open up?"

"Soon as I can find some furniture and get a sign made. I talked to the drummer from Chattanooga at breakfast this morning and ordered some medicine and things I'll be needing. He promised to have it shipped on the next freight wagon coming this way."

"In case you can't cure your customers, it shore will be convenient having the undertaker right next door," Shiloh said, slapping Doc on the shoulder.

"Hadn't thought of that," Doc said, chuckling.

"Lester just drug in. He had a hard night. He's trying to get some sleep right now. I'm gonna mosey down to the sheriff's office. I'll see you after awhile."

Shiloh met and spoke to several folks as he strode down the boardwalk. The single word over the door read *Sherriff.* Shiloh pushed inside.

Sam Potter had been the sheriff of Monroe County ever since Shiloh could remember. He was getting on up in years now. His gray hair and deep wrinkles told of too many trips down too many roads. Right now he was tilted back in a chair, his booted feet resting on top of a dilapidated desk, sipping coffee.

"Nathan Whittington, ain't it?" the old sheriff asked, peering over the rim of his cup. "I heard you was back in town. You been gone a spell, boy."

"Yes sir. Something over four years I reckon."

"Don't know exactly what you done to the judge, but you shore got him riled up. He stormed in here yesterday hopping mad. He was bound and determined for me to arrest you and throw away the key. He never could tell me any law you broke. Might ought to walk easy around him for awhile. He's got a long memory and some mighty powerful friends."

"I can't prove it, but I figure Abe Sawyer's one of 'em" Shiloh said, spinning a chair and straddling it. "They're using the law to steal land that decent folks have worked their whole lives for. But then, I figure you already know what's going on don't you, Sheriff?"

"If you're asking do I know they're not crossing the T's and dotting the I's on those tax sales by not advertising them, the answer is yes. But I don't know any law they're breaking. If you're asking if I'm in cahoots with Abe Sawyer or on his payroll, the answer is no.

"I made a big mistake by being pressured into hiring those two, so-called, deputies. I should have known better. I'm an old man, Nathan. I've been the sheriff here in Monroe County over twenty years. I don't know nothing else.

"I've got a lot of good friends here in the valley. Your pa was one of them. I'm shore sorry about what happened to your folks. Wish I knew who the low down dirty skunk was that give the Yanks that list I'd—"

"Sheriff Potter!" a terrified voice from outside shouted. "Sheriff Potter!"

The door burst open. A young fellow with a look of terror on his face ran into the office.

"Come quick, Sheriff!" he said breathlessly. "It's Miss Elizabeth— something terrible has happened!"

Shiloh was out of the chair and through the door before the sheriff could get up. The young boy ran before him. Up ahead, at the edge of town, Shiloh could see several folks gathered in front of the little white house with a picket fence around it. It was Elizabeth's house.

Two women on the front porch were hugging each other and crying. Shiloh pushed past two men standing in the doorway. Someone pointed to the bedroom. He bounded across the living room and through the bedroom door.

She lay sprawled facedown cross the bed. Blood was everywhere. He rushed to her side. She lay deathly still.

"Don't move her till the Doc gets here," somebody suggested.

"What happened?" Shiloh shouted to no one and everyone.

"When she didn't open the store this morning, Mrs. Jacobs came to check on her and found her like that," some fellow said.

Doc limped up with his black bag. He kneeled beside the bed and placed a finger against her neck. Seconds ticked by. Doc's face took on a grim look.

"She's still alive but barely," he said. "Let's roll her over. Easy now."

Shiloh gasped when her face came into view. It was a swollen bloody mass of torn flesh and bruises. He would not even have recognized her. The sheriff pushed breathlessly into the room, took one look and began shooing everybody out.

Doc took long minutes gently touching her sides, stomach, and chest.

The look on his face told Shiloh what he didn't want to know.

"She's all broken up inside," Doc finally said, shaking his head sadly.

"Somebody's beat this lady to a pulp. There's just nothing I can do."

Shiloh's stomach knotted at the words. A lump in his throat wouldn't swallow back down. Tears washed his eyes. An overwhelming tide of anger swamped over him.

"Hold on," Doc said. "She's coming around."

A swollen eye pried open to a thin slit and swept weakly from side to side, searching, coming to rest on Shiloh's face. Her torn lips moved and mouthed silent words. Shiloh bent closer. The Sheriff was there beside him.

"Who done this, Miss Elizabeth?" he asked, anger evident in his voice.

Again her lips moved and formed a single word. "Roy."

Shiloh's hand went to her battered face in a tender touch. Her one swollen eye met his concerned gaze. Her mouth moved. Shiloh leaned an ear close.

"The list," she said in a slurred whisper. "It was Roy. He bragged while he beat me."

Shiloh flicked a quick glance at the sheriff. He nodded that he had heard, that it was all he needed to hear. He pushed to his feet and stomped angrily from the room.

"Don't talk," Shiloh whispered to Elizabeth. "You need to rest."

She rolled her head weakly from side to side. Pain masked her face. Large silver tears escaped her eyes.

"Let her talk if she wants," Doc said softly. "She ain't got long."

Shiloh bent close. His lips gently touched hers.

"I love you," her lips formed the words.

She sucked several short gasps through swollen lips, then let out a long escape of air from her lungs. Her eye closed . . .and Shiloh's heart stopped.

"She's gone, son," Doc said, touching Shiloh on the shoulder. "She's not hurting anymore."

He felt the soul-deep sear of agonizing grief blossom in his chest. Huge sobs pushed up his throat and wracked his body. His muscles trembled and his heart battered around inside his chest.

He collapsed to sit on the floor beside the bed, burying his face in both hands. He felt as if his whole world had just ended.

They rode in near sundown. Most everyone in town stopped what they were doing and stood silently on front porches, on the boardwalk, or stopped in the street to gaze at the little procession. Tiny tendrils of dust lifted with each step of their horse's hooves and puffed away, swept eastward by a hot wind.

Sheriff Potter led the way on his Zebra dun sitting straight and tall in his saddle. Behind him rode the tall deputy. His coat pulled back behind the pistol tied low on his left leg. Next came the big, burly deputy. In his hand he held the reins to a sorrel gelding trailing behind his own mount. Slung belly down across the saddle was the body of Roy Clymer.

"They got him!" somebody shouted. "They got the murdering skunk."

Shiloh, Doc, and Lester stood on the boardwalk in front of the undertaker's office. Beside them stood Elizabeth's father and mother.

The next few days were a blur in Shiloh's mind. His body moved through the motions in a tranced state.

Roy Clymer was buried early the next morning in an unmarked grave beside his folks. No one but the undertaker and the sheriff were present.

Most everybody in the whole valley attended Elizabeth's funeral the following afternoon. The little church house was packed and as many more folks stood outside, unable to get in. Shiloh couldn't have told you a word the reverend said if his life depended upon it. He stood beside Mr. and Mrs. Johnson at the graveside and listened without hearing as the preacher said something about dust to dust and ashes to ashes. He watched without seeing as the pretty wooden casket was lowered.

Folks in the whole valley depended on the mercantile store for their supplies. Since Roy's folks had passed on and there were no known Clymer heirs, the judge ruled both the store and Elizabeth's home belonged to her folks.. Their first act was to tear down the Clymer Mercantile sign and replace it with one that simply read, *Sweetwater General Store*. Their second act was to sell the store to Shiloh and Lester.

"I wouldn't be no hand at running a store," Ben Johnson told Shiloh.

"I've raised cattle and farmed my whole life. I'm too old to change horses in the middle of the stream."

"If you're sure that's what you want to do," Shiloh said. "Me and Lester have talked about it and we'd like to buy it from you. I'm kind of like you, I wouldn't be no good at it either, but Lester is real excited about it and we're gonna go in partners. I'll help him until he gets the hang of it."

"Then we've got a deal." Ben said, sticking out a hand to seal the bargain. "That young lawyer, Clayton Moore? He's buying Elizabeth's house. I'll have him go ahead and draw up the papers on the store while he's at it."

Doc's new practice kept him running his legs off. About the only time they got to see him was come suppertime at the boarding house where they all still lived. He bought the little black buggy that had been sitting at the livery for the past two years since doctor Adams died. Most days he was gone, making house calls in the valley, doctoring sick folks. Shiloh couldn't figure out what they all done before the Doc came.

Shiloh and Lester worked from sunup till sundown at the store. They discovered it wasn't just a store. It was the hub of the whole community. They handled everything from feed and seed to women's corsets.

Shiloh cracked a grin, for the first time in nearly two weeks since Elizabeth's death, the day Lester sold Mrs. Bellworth some ladies undergarments.

"What are you grinning about?" Lester demanded, after the heavyset woman had left. "You get to wait on the next woman that wants to buy something like that."

"Not on your life," Shiloh said, barely able to keep from laughing out loud. "Corsets and such are your department."

Most every night after supper, Shiloh strolled down to the creek and sat for an hour or so under the old weeping willow tree. The moonlight reflecting on the water, the soft breeze whispering through the willow leaves, the solitude of the place, all gave him a feeling of Elizabeth's nearness.He would toss a small pebble into the dark water and watch the ripples spread out in all directions. Then he would take the memory of their last night together from his mind . . .and love her all over again.

It was two weeks to the day since the tragic events, when Sheriff Trotter came by the store. Lester had gone to deliver a wagonload of feed and Shiloh was alone.

"Morning, Sheriff," Shiloh greeted.

"Howdy, Nath," the sheriff said. "I still can't get use to calling you Shiloh like your friends do."

"Don't matter none. I reckon I've answered to a lot of names over the years. Most of the boys in my cavalry outfit called me Tennessee for the first year or so."

"How's the store coming? Seems to me you boys are doing right well."

"Lester's liking it but I'm kind of tolerating," Shiloh told him. "I never did hear where you caught up with Roy that day?"

"We tracked him north to Maryville. He was sitting in a watering hole crying in his beer as usual. He never could stay away from the booze or women. I figure the guilt of giving the Yankees that list was eating his insides. Some folks had been whispering that he might be slapping Elizabeth around but she wouldn't admit it and I didn't have any proof."

"What happened? How'd he get all shot up like that? The undertaker said he had five bullet holes in him."

"Well, it ain't something I've talked about, but since you asked, I reckon you got a right to know. He was just sitting there at a table by himself knocking back one drink after another when we walked in. I told him he was under arrest and he started to stand up. Before I knowed what was happening, Utah, that gun-slick deputy, whipped out his pistol and put five shots into Roy quicker than you could say scat.

"Truth of it is, I should've arrested him for murder right on the spot. He claimed he thought Roy was going for a gun. Turned out, Roy wasn't even carrying one. A few years ago I would have arrested him. Years does something to a man. Takes the salt out of his backbone I reckon.

"I tried to fire both of them when we got back. Told them I wanted their badges. They just laughed at me. Can you believe it? They laughed at me and called me a pathetic old has been. . .and I stood there and took it."

"You gonna let it go at that?" Shiloh asked.

"What else can I do?" Sam asked, helplessness sounding in his voice. "I can't brace those two by myself. I wouldn't stand a chance."

Without a word Shiloh ripped the apron from around his waist and slung it on the counter. Bending, he lifted his gun rig from under the counter and strapped it on. He tied the leg strap and adjusted the holster into its familiar position.

"Deputize me," Shiloh told the sheriff.

"Wha—what are you talking about?"

"Deputize me. We're going to fire a couple of deputies."

"Now wait a minute, boy," the sheriff said. "I ain't asking you to fight my battles."

"You want to get shed of them or not? You want them and Abe Sawyer running this whole valley? Cause that's what's gonna happen unless you stand up to them. I ain't meaning to fight your battles but I don't want to live in a town with them running it. Now you gonna deputize me or not?"

"If you're willing, I'm ready. Let's go over and have the judge witness me swearing you in. That way they can't come back on us later in case something goes wrong."

A stiff westerly breeze gathered clouds of dust and sent it swirling between rows of clapboard buildings that lined the single street of Sweetwater. The sun hung high as Sheriff Potter and Shiloh strode side by side down the middle of the dusty street. Both wore shiny badges displayed prominently on their chests. The sheriff carried a sawed off double-barreled shotgun in the crook of his arm.

Townspeople saw and knew something was happening. Small groups of two's and three's gathered, questioned each other, then followed at a safe distance.

The batwing doors made a soft squeaking sound as Sheriff Potter and Shiloh pushed into the saloon. Shiloh swept the room with a quick glance. Only eight men were in the room. Five sat hunched over a poker table, their eyes intent on the cards in their hands.

The bartender he remembered from his first visit was pouring another round for the only other customers, the two deputies. The big fellow said something to his partner, who cast an inquiring glance over his shoulder.

Shiloh shifted casually to one side, moving several steps away from the sheriff. If it came down to a shooting, he wanted to have them in crossfire.

"Utah," Sheriff Potter said in a firm, unwavering voice. "You're under arrest for the murder of Roy Clymer. Keep your hands where I can see em."

A deathly hush settled over the room.

The burly one, the sheriff called him Jessup, turned to face the sheriff and stepped away from his partner a couple of steps. His right hand dropped casually to his side, only inches from the Remington he wore.

Utah continued to lean on the bar, twisting only his head to fix a cold stare at the sheriff. One corner of his lips curled, forming only a hint of a mocking smile. His right hand lifted the shot glass of golden liquid to his lips, sipping it gingerly as he continued to stare.

"Unbuckle your gun belt and let it drop to the floor. We can do this the easy way or the hard way. Your choice."

"Go away, old man," Utah muttered. "You're starting to annoy me."

The metallic double click sound of both hammers of the sheriff's shotgun being pulled back echoed loud in the deathly stillness of the room.

Shiloh's intense gaze remained fixed on the big man.

"I never tell a man the same thing twice," the sheriff said, spreading his feet. You got just three heartbeats left in this world unless I see that pistol hit the floor."

"Okay, old man," Utah whispered. "You got the drop on me this time. But this ain't the end of it."

"Then maybe I oughtta just blow you out of your boots and get it over and done with."

Straightening, the deputy raised his left gun hand in the air. His right hand lowered slowly, reached across his body to the leg cord on his left leg and untied it. Then his hand moved upward to unbuckle his gun belt and let it drop.

"You...! Jessup," the sheriff said. "You're next. Right easy like. Let's hear it hit the floor."

There was no hesitation. Jessup carefully unbuckled his belt and let his gun rig drop. A mixture of fear and hatred occupied his eyes.

"Now I want those badges. Lay 'em on the bar," Sheriff Potter said. "It's a disgrace for the likes of you to wear a deputy's badge."

They did as he said, both boring holes in him with a gaze.

"Jessup," the sheriff said. "You've done wore out your welcome in Sweetwater. I figure it'll take me about five minutes to get Utah locked up. Soon as I do, I'm gonna come looking for you. You'd be smart to be on your horse heading somewhere before then. Now you better git before I change my mind."

He got. By the time they marched Utah up to the jail and locked him in, they heard the sound of a galloping horse heading south out of town.

"Shore appreciate you siding me awhile ago," Sam said to Shiloh, hanging the jail keys on a peg beside the door.

"You didn't need my help, Sheriff," Shiloh told him. "Don't know how you could have handled it any better."

"It felt good. I reckon just you being there backing me was what I needed. To be honest with you Nathan, it's been awhile since I felt good about wearing this badge. I done made up my mind though, as long as it's pinned on my chest, things are gonna be different around here."

"Well, I better be getting back to the store," Shiloh said over his shoulder as he headed for the door. "You done a good job, Sheriff."

"I'm obliged to you," Sheriff Potter called after him.

The trial was held on July 21, 1865, two weeks after Utah was arrested. Despite efforts by Abe Sawyer to get his hired gun released, Sheriff Potter had steadfastly refused to let him out of jail until the trial.

Clayton Moore, the new young lawyer in town, was hired by Sawyer to defend his man. Since the county didn't have a prosecuting attorney, Sheriff Potter had to present the case against the accused.

From the start, it was clear the fix was in. The judge picked the jury, choosing mostly those on Abe Sawyer's payroll. The trail lasted less than an hour and the jury didn't even leave their seats before finding him not guilty.

Shiloh pushed from his chair and patted the old sheriff on the shoulder. His gaze locked for a moment with that of Clayton Moore. The young lawyer dropped his head, clearly not proud of what had just happened.

"I'd say you better watch your back for awhile," Shiloh told Sheriff Potter.

"Yeah," Sam agreed dejectedly, "that might be good advice for both of us."

Utah and one of Abe Sawyer's men left the courtroom together, talking and laughing. The gunman's cold eyes cut a look over his shoulder at Shiloh, its meaning crystal clear.

Three days passed without incident. A showdown would come; it was just a matter of time. Shiloh knew Utah wasn't the kind to just let bygones be bygones. Uneasiness gnawed at Shiloh. He jumped at every sound. Every sudden movement he caught out of the corner of his eye caused his stomach to knot and his hand to flash toward the pistol on his hip.

It was near noon. The July sun was blazing hot. Shiloh was helping the freight driver unload a shipment of feed when he saw one of Abe Sawyer's men coming. From the smirking look pasted on the fellow's face Shiloh knew within himself the waiting was over.

"I got a message for you from Utah," the cocky fellow said, hooking his thumbs inside his gun belt. "He said to tell you, you was a yellow livered Reb coward and didn't have the nerve to meet him face to face without the sheriff and his scatter gun. He said he'd be waiting in front of the saloon at twelve o'clock."

The man curled a satisfied grin and turned on his heels. For a long minute Shiloh stared at the man's back as he walked away, turning once to glance back and laugh. Lester had just walked out the back door of the store with a letter in his hand and heard the message.

"Tell me you ain't thinking about going," Lester told his friend. "From all I hear, he's a gunfighter and cold blooded killer. I've watched you practice night after night. You're fast, no doubt about it, but you'd be no match for that fellow."

"Unless you got another snake up your sleeve I don't see I got a choice," Shiloh said, untying the apron from around his waist and heading inside.

"I came out to tell you, you got a letter here from John Walters," Lester told him, following him into the store.

"I'll read it after I've done what I gotta do," Shiloh told his friend. "First things first."

Shiloh strode over and pulled his gun rig from under the counter. He buckled it in place, tied the leg cord, and checked to make sure it was fully loaded. He rolled up his sleeves as he glanced up at the big clock on the wall— eight minutes until twelve.

He turned to stare into the face of the best friend he'd ever had. He saw concern written there. He stuck out his hand. It was taken. For a brief space of time they felt each other's firm handclasp.

"If this don't turn out good," Shiloh told his friend. "My land is yours. You know where the rest of the money is, split it between you and Doc. You're all the family I got."

"You don't have to do this," Lester said, swallowing hard and blinking to hold back tears.

"Yeah, I do, Lester. Yeah, I do."

The word had already spread like wildfire. People lined the boardwalk on both sides of the street. Just like the battle of the bayonets, Shiloh thought as he stepped into the dusty street, only with different weapons.

Sheriff Potter hurried up the street to intercept him. His double barrel nested in the crook of his arm and a worried look occupied his face.

"Let me handle it," he said, as he stopped in front of Shiloh.

"No," Shiloh told him. "I'm the one he called out. Besides, he ain't broke the law."

"I could run him out of town just on general principals. Ain't no use getting yourself killed."

"Sheriff, ever since that sham trial, I've jumped every time the cat meowed. I hate living like that. Might as well get it settled and done."

"Well, the least I can do is make sure he's the only one that takes a hand in it. I'll keep an eye on your back."

"Thanks, Sheriff. Can't think of nobody I'd rather have watching my back."

He moved down the middle of the street with measured strides. He was aware of, but ignored the dozens of people that lined the street. His gaze fixed straight ahead on the man leaning against a post in front of the saloon.

Shiloh stopped forty feet shy of the saloon, spreading his feet slightly, his hands hanging loosely at his sides.

"I heard you wanted to see me," he said in a loud whisper.

"I didn't figure you had the guts to show up," Utah sipping slowly from a shot glass in his right hand and peered at Shiloh. "Being a yellow dog, Rebel like you are."

"You gonna talk, drink, or fight?" Shiloh asked evenly.

"You're anxious to die ain't you, Reb?"

"No," Shiloh said. "I'm anxious to rid the world of vermin like you."

Utah's eyes narrowed a notch to thin slits. He threw back his head and drained the glass, cast it aside, and stepped into the dusty street.

Shiloh saw the man's eyes flick up to the big clock on the front of the courthouse. His own gaze traveled that way. Two minutes till noon.

"When the clock strikes, I'm gonna kill you," the gunfighter said, matter-of-factly.

Utah fingered the left side of his coat back behind his pistol. His hand fluttered and twitched just above the pearl handled Colt in a cutaway holster, like a dragonfly over a pond. Shiloh licked his lips and bent his knees slightly, shifting his feet to a comfortable position. His muscles tensed.

They stood facing each other, forty feet apart. Their unwavering stares fixed. The wind whistled. Small swirls of dust lapped at the feet of both combatants. Somewhere a horse snorted. A dog barked. The clock struck.

Like a streak of greased lightning, between one breath and the next, Utah's left hand swept upward, the pistol appeared as if by magic in his fist. The nose began its arch upward. Two explosions sounded. A bullet plowed a furrow at the gunfighter's feet. Shiloh watched, as the pistol tilted downward, then dropped from a weakened hand to the ground at Utah's feet. The man's right hand clutched at his stomach. Blood gushed between his fingers. He pulled it away, gazing at his blood-soaked hand, his eyes walled white in disbelief. Great drops of his life liquid dropped into the dusty street, forming tiny red mudballs where they landed.

Blue-black gun smoke trailed upward from the pistol Shiloh still clutched in his hand. The smoke burned his nostrils. Utah toppled face forward into the street. Shiloh holstered his weapon and turned away, striding back toward the store.

CHAPTER VII

"You got any idea when you'll be back?" Lester asked, as him and Doc watched Shiloh check his pack mule again.

"No idea," Shiloh replied. "I've never been to Mexico, but I hear it's a big country."

"I don't understand how you're gonna find the colonel in a big country like that."

"All I know is what John Walters told me in his letter. He said after they discovered the colonel had been stealing all that money and they were gonna court-martial him, he lit out with a dozen of his men. The army caught up with them and there was a fight. Four of the colonel's men were killed another two were captured. One of the ones they captured was the Bear.

"John said when faced with a court martial and a firing squad, he starting singing like a mocking bird. He told them the colonel knew about a place somewhere in western Mexico, he didn't know exactly where. That's where they were headed."

"Shore hate to see you go, Shiloh," Doc told him, their hands gripping hard in unsaid things. "I've kind of got use to having you around."

"I can't rightly explain it, so it makes sense. It's just something I've got to do before I can get on with my life. You boys take care of things."

Shiloh toed a stirrup and pulled into the saddle. He double-wrapped the lead rope to his new pack mule, then reined his buckskin around and kneed him forward. An odd feeling of sadness settled in his stomach.

Twisting in the saddle as he rode down the street, Shiloh's gaze lingered for a space of time on his two friends standing there together. He realized full well that this might be the last time that he ever saw them. He lifted a gloved finger to his old floppy cavalry hat, then quickly turned his head away, not wanting his friends to see his dampening eyes.

The big buckskin seemed anxious to stretch his legs. He high-stepped sideways, tugging at the reins. Shiloh returned a scattering of howdies with a slow nod of his head. Busy townspeople paused for a moment, watched, lifted hands, then went on about their work. Kate Solesbee paused from sweeping the front porch of the boarding house as he rode by.

"You hurry back, now," she called out in her boisterous voice. "You hear?"

Shiloh offered a smile and a two-fingered touch to his hat. These are good folks, he thought. Maybe someday, when this was all over, he could settle down here and feel like this was home again. Maybe someday.

The date was August 6, 1865 when Shiloh rode slowly down the busy street of El Paso, Texas. He was trail weary. He'd been polishing his saddle for over two months since he left Sweetwater. He needed to sleep in a real bed for a change and took note of the hotel as he passed.

His face fixed straight ahead, but his searching eyes flicked from side to side, exploring every sight, absorbing every sound, searching every face. His two months on the trail had taught him to be suspicions of everyone and everything.

Crossing half the country, purposely avoiding towns, he had kept to himself, becoming a loner. He made his camps well off any trail and stopped at a town only when he needed to replenish his trail supplies.. Nonetheless, in Arkansas he had a shootout with two would-be highwaymen, killing one and wounding the other. In the badlands of Oklahoma territory, Indians had tried unsuccessfully to relieve him of his horse and pack mule on two occasions.

He had ridden through the desolate wastelands of New Mexico and had a run-in with a pack of Comanchero. He had survived, and picked up a pair of bone handled Colts in the process. Now, he had ridden clear across Texas, which seemed to him as large as the rest of the country put together, and fought the Apache for the privilege. He had survived only because his buckskin was better horseflesh than their inferior mustang, Indian ponies. At last, only a wide, muddy river separated him from Mexico.

Reining up at the open double doors of a livery, he swung stiffly from the saddle. His booted foot touched the ground and it seemed foreign to him. His gloved hand held on to the saddle horn until his feet and legs adjusted to the unfamiliar stance.

"Looks like you've come far, stranger," the grizzled old liveryman said, spitting a stream of tobacco juice to accent his observation.

"Yeah," Shiloh breathed hoarsely, the words barely coming out in a raspy whisper. "How could you tell?"

"Your horse and mule are trail sore. I could tell it when you rode in. See how their ankles are swollen. They're needing a rest."

"So am I," Shiloh told him, loosening cinch straps and slinging his saddlebags across a shoulder.

"See they get plenty of grain and a stall with fresh hay."

"I can shore do that, mister. A dollar a day for the both of 'em and I'll have 'em fit and frisky when you get ready to ride on. Want me to store your gear and saddle guns too? Don't mind me saying so, you're packing enough hardware to start the war all over again. I ain't seen one of those Sharps buffalo guns around these parts in quite a spell, and that sawed off Stevens double barrel hanging there on your saddle is enough to scare the life out of a fellow."

"Yeah, I'd be obliged," Shiloh told him, digging a five dollar half-eagle from his pocket and flipping it to the old timer. "You happen to notice a half dozen hardcases ride through here a couple or three months back, maybe heading into Mexico?"

"There's lots of hardcases ride through here," the old man said, scratching his whiskers and thinking hard. "Yeah . . .now that you mention it, there was a bunch rode through about then. They stopped for a couple of days, then headed across the river. I recollect cause one of em's horse went lame and I sold him another. His had a U. S. brand on it. Like to never got shed of a Yankee horse in Reb country."

"They didn't happen to mention where they were headed, did they?"

"Not that I can recall," the holster said, spitting another stream of juice. "They stayed over at the hotel though. Miss Sarah runs it. She might know something. She makes it her business to know might near everything that goes on around these parts."

"Thanks, I'm obliged," Shiloh said, turning on his heels and heading back up the street.

The El Paso hotel, as the sign read, was a two-story adobe structure. A small, second story balcony overlooked the street. He pushed through the open door.

He assumed the plump lady with the well-endowed bosom and painted face was the Miss Sarah, the old holster had referred to. She looked like ten pounds of woman poured into a five pound sack. She stood behind the counter, fanning her sweaty face with a cardboard fan. Her eyes lifted and a wide smile washed across her face as he strode in.

"Something I can do for you, handsome?" she asked, letting her eyes slowly drift up and down his six foot four inch frame a couple of times.

"If you got a room overlooking the street, you can," he told her in a hoarse whisper.

"I got eight rooms, all empty. You can take your pick," she said, reaching a key from under the counter. Her dark eyes engaged his as she handed it to him.

"Is there anything else I can do for you?" she said, slanting another smile.

"Maybe there is," he said, "Two or three months ago a half-dozen fellows rode through. I understand they stayed here a couple of nights. One of them was a big fellow, walks straight up, kind of like he's better than anybody else. Wears a scar on his left cheek, most likely goes by the title of Colonel. You remember anybody like that?"

"Suppose I do?" she asked, suddenly becoming businesslike. "What's it worth?"

Shiloh fished a half-eagle from his pocket and held it up for her to see. Her gaze flicked to it, then back up at him. She reached for it.

"Uh-uh," he said, making the coin disappear into his fist. "Not until I hear what you got to say."

"They were here. Stayed two days. Tighter than Dick's hatband, they were. All except Wilbur, now he was nice. He knew how to treat a lady."

"Did Wilbur happen to say where they were headed by any chance?"

"No," she said. "He didn't talk much. He was . . .out of breath most of the time. He did ask me once how far it was to Chihuahua, Mexico."

"What did you tell him?" he asked, handing her the coin.

"How should I know how far it is, I've never been across the river and I got no hankering to go."

"Where could a fellow get a hot bath, a shave, and a haircut around here?"

"Next street over about halfway up. They got bath stalls behind the barbershop. But, I've got a bathtub in my room. I could even scrub your back if you like," she said in a low, husky voice.

"Thanks anyway," he told her, "I'm kind of short winded."

He found his room and pushed into it. It was mostly empty. Only a small bed, which was little more than a cot, one straight-back, hide bottom chair, a rickety table and a water pitcher sitting in a tin basin. Faded and dusty curtains with rotted holes leaked light through the single window.

Strolling over, he parted them with a finger and inspected the outside balcony with a slow sweep of his eyes. Turning, he felt the bed and wasn't at all surprised to find it lumpy. It was about the sorriest looking hotel room he had ever seen. He hung his saddlebags over the chair and locked the door behind him before tromping down the stairs. He figured Miss Sarah must have given up on him because she barely looked at him as he left.

After a steaming hot bath, a shave, and getting shed of a month's growth of hair, he felt like a new man. On the way back to a little eating place he had seen earlier, he passed a leather shop. On an impulse, he turned in. A small Mexican fellow greeted him with a smile.

He had thoughts of buying another holster for the matching pistols he had taken off the Comanchero that didn't need them anymore. He now wore its twin on his right hip. The man had dozens of fine crafted holsters, gunbelts, saddles, and all kind of leather goods.

His gaze fell on a holster rig like he had never seen before. It was a left handed belly holster built as a part of the matching cartridge belt. It intrigued him. He bought it.

"Could you make me a leather roll-up with six compartments that would hold a bayonet?" he asked the man. "I'll also need a scabbard for one to wear on my belt."

"Si señor," the fellow said, smiling. "If it is made of leather I can make it."

Shiloh explained in detail what he wanted, made arrangements that it would be ready the day after tomorrow, and paid the man. Leaving the shop, he stood aside to allow a poor looking Mexican peon leading a burro to pass. Behind the half starved burro was a small two-wheeled cart loaded down with adobe bricks. Something touched Shiloh's heart as his gaze followed the man.

"Señor," Shiloh called out.

The fellow turned his head to the sound. Sad eyes stared out from under a worn out straw sombrero. He wore a tattered, woven serape over pants and shirt that used to be white. His face showed a questioning look.

"Si, señor?" the fellow asked. "You wish to buy my bricks?"

"No," Shiloh told him. "I want to buy your serape. Will twenty dollars be enough for it?" Shiloh handed the man a gold double eagle.

A puzzled look washed over the Mexican's dark, weathered face. He glanced down at the worn out serape he wore, then back at the crazy Americano that was offering to buy it. The puzzled look changed to sadness.

"That is too much, señor," he said. "You could buy many new ones for less."

"I know. But I would like to have that one."

The sad look on the fellow's face suddenly changed to surprise, then to happiness. He swiped the hat from his head and quickly shrugged out of the serape, handing it to Shiloh before he backed out.

The Mexican's dark eyes lit up when Shiloh handed him the shiny new twenty dollar gold piece. He offered a huge smile and bent from the waist.

"Gracias, señor. Muchas gracias."

Shiloh had a good feeling down inside as he headed down the street, carrying his serape, to the little eating place. Somebody's cooking besides his own would go down right well. A couple days rest for him and his animals before he crossed into Mexico shore wouldn't hurt nothing either.

CHAPTER VIII

The small Mexican village had no street, only openings between the two dozen or so, scattered adobe hovels that hugged a sloping hillside.

The boiling sun hung high. It had long since stolen all but the most meager patches of shade.

A half-dozen gaunt red chickens cocked their heads from their picking in the sand and scolded the rider, then fled in a flurry of dust from their batting wings as they scurried from the path of the sweat-soaked, high stepping buckskin.

Little plumes of dust puffed away from the horse's hooves, swept eastward by a hot, dry wind that flung stinging particles of sand before it. A local peon bent into it. He clung to his ragged sombrero with one hand and to a half starved burro with the other. For a long moment he paused and peered through squinted eyes at the gringo on the big horse, then hurried on his way.

Shiloh sat straight and tall in the saddle. A faded serape draped across his wide shoulders, its ragged edges fluttered in the driving wind. The buckskin's reins were held comfortably in his gloved hand, like they were born there. His right hand rested easily on his lap, scant inches from the bone handled Colt in the greased holster tied low on his right leg. Its twin rode unseen in a belly holster, hidden from sight by the covering he wore.

His features were lost under a month's stubble of beard that failed to disguise the hard-set mouth and pale green eyes: hard eyes that peered from under a battered Confederate cavalry hat, riding low on his forehead, eyes that had grown cold and suspicious in the past few months, eyes that squeezed tight against the sear of the wind but flicked like lightning from a dark thunderstorm and took in every detail of the jumble of buildings.

He rode past, but seemed to mostly ignore, a small mud hut with a pole arbor along the front. A jumbled assortment of colorful blankets in striped orange, yellow, and red flapped wildly from the poles. A long strand of red peppers hung in bunches. Straw sombreros were stacked on a plank stretched between two wooden barrels and weighted down with a rock.

Up ahead, his searching look revealed an old mission. Its heavy wooden doors shut tightly against the stifling heat and blowing sand. Its bell tower lorded high above the lowly village like a sentinel keeping vigil over its own. The bell, pushed by the wind, emitted a soft, rhythmic ring.

A furrow plowed across Shiloh's brow and shock pushed aside disbelief when his gaze fell upon a dug well in front of the mission. A well?

How could that be? He pointed his buckskins nose in that direction.

He stretched his full frame high in the stirrups before drifting a leg over the saddle and bringing himself stiffly down and planting a worn boot in the hot, white sand.

Dropping his reins at the buckskin's feet, he stepped to the rock parapet that surrounded the well. Wearing a puzzled look, he peered down into the bowels of the earth. The darkness swallowed his vision. He shook his head in wonderment how anyone could, or would, dig a well out here in the middle of the desert. This place was a long ride from anywhere.

Taking up the roped, wooden bucket, he lowered it into the well. Fifty feet of rope played out before he heard a pleasing splash. He felt the pressure when it filled, then hand over hand, drew the precious liquid to light.

He dumped the contents in the small horse trough beside the rock wall. The big gelding's nostrils flared. He dipped his nose and with long, slurping sounds, quickly drank the trough dry.

He reached for the gourd dipper hanging by a rawhide thong, ladled it full from the second bucket and lifted it to his cracked lips. He cautiously took a sip. Startled, he pulled the dipper away and stared a long moment at the sweetest, coldest, purest tasting water he had ever put to his lips.

Dipper after dipper he drank, long and slow, letting it trickle down his parched throat, cooked that way by two months in the blistering Mexican sun. Out of water two days, he had sustained both himself and the buckskin by squeezing the tart liquid from the garambulla cactus dotting the desert.

After several more buckets, both his and the buckskins thirst had been slaked. Only then, did his gaze examine closer the remainder of the buildings and felt pleasure when he identified the one next to the mission as a small cantina. He headed there.

Striding through the open doorway, he paused, and swept the room with a quick glance as had become his custom. His look revealed four tables with mismatching chairs and a small, makeshift bar. A faded blanket partially covered an opening leading to another room from which wafted the overpowering aroma of Mexican food. He was way past hungry. He scraped a chair across the hardpacked sand floor and settled into it.

"Buenas tardes, señor," a pudgy little Mexican with a friendly face greeted as he hurried up.

The smallish, middle aged fellow had more hair in his mustache than he did on his balding head. He was heavy around the middle, like he had been enjoying too much of his own cooking. The smile that washed his face looked genuine, not the usual faked substitute he had grown accustomed to during his two months south of the border.

"Buenas tardes," he replied, his own voice sounding strange, unused for more than awhile. The words came out raspy, barely more than a whisper. "Do you understand English?"

"Si, señor," the man said. "I understand."

"Good," Shiloh whispered. "I need a heaping plateful of whatever you got back there and a cup of coffee to wash it down. Then bag me up something I can take with me for a few days. I'd be obliged."

"Si, señor," the man replied, swiping thick dust from the table with a rag, before hurrying toward the opening to the back room.

Accident, or maybe pure old luck, had caused him to stumble onto the remote village. His pack mule had come up lame after being bitten by a sidewinder a week after leaving Chihuahua. For the better part of three weeks he had lived off the land, and in this country, the land gave up mighty little. He figured whatever he was smelling from the back room would be an improvement on the rattlesnake, desert blue quail, and the single javelina wild hog he had managed to kill.

"Buenas tardes, señor," a sweet sounding voice said from behind him. "Your food will be ready quickly."

Jerking a look, he saw maybe the most beautiful señorita he had ever laid a gaze upon. No bigger than a good hiccup, her angelic face was soft and olive color. Her dark, dancing eyes matched the pretty smile on her perfectly shaped lips. Straight black hair hung well below a tiny waist. A red, ankle length skirt touched the tops of woven straw sandals. The white blouse, gathered at the top, offered only the slightest hint of the youthful breasts and caused a man to wonder about the rest. She looked to be in her late teens.

"I am Consuela." the girl said in near perfect English.

"Buenas tardes, señorita Consuela," he said in a loud whisper. "Some call me Shiloh."

His admiring gaze followed her as she set a coffee cup before him and filled it from a blackened pot she then set on the table. As she did, their eyes met, and held for a long moment. Seemingly reading his thoughts, a knowing smile lifted one corner of her pretty lips as she straightened.

"How is it you speak English so well?" he asked.

"Father Sebastian is the priest in our village. He is an Americano. He taught me to speak your language when I was very young. He established our village many years ago. It was he that dug the well to God's water."

"God's water?" Shiloh asked, feeling a puzzled look overtake his face. "What's that?"

"That is what we call the water from the well. It is also the name of our village, señor." She said, flipping her head sideways to fling the hair behind her bare shoulder. "El Aqua Dios, God's water. The padre came to our country when he was a young man to establish a mission. He wandered through the desert for many months before reaching this place. Here, he fell into a trance from exhaustion and thirst.

"A passing goat herder found him and gave him water. When he awoke, he believed it a sign from God and that this was the place to which he had been divinely led. The nearest water was many days walk away. The next day he began digging the well with nothing more than his hands.

"The desert people heard about it and thought him insane at first. Soon, one by one, they came to help. They grew to believe so strongly, they built the mission even before the well was completed. It is said one day they lowered the worker to continue digging and discovered it full of water.

"They believed it a miracle. Father Sebastian said God's water was there all along, it just took someone willing to be used as an instrument to remove the barrier. Now, God's water can be enjoyed by all."

"Well, if that don't beat all," Shiloh whispered.

"Excuse me, señor, I will see if father has your food ready."

Shiloh's look followed her as she glided smoothly across the room. He was fascinated how she carried herself for one so young. While she was gone, he mulled over the story she had told and shook his head in amazement.

Draining the last swig from his cup, he refilled it from the pot on the table. He didn't know if he believed in miracles or not. He sure didn't know what it took to qualify as one. One thing for shore, digging a fifty-foot well in the middle of the desert and finding water had to be mighty close.

He was still considering the story when Consuela broke into his thoughts, setting a plate of steaming Mexican food before him. Lowering his face, he drew in a deep sniffer full of the hot, spicy aroma and let his breath out in a slow slide of air. How long had it been since he sat down to a meal like that? Way too long.

"Would you have a cup with me?" he asked, noticing the empty cup in her hand.

"Si, gracias, señor," she said, smiling sweetly and melting gracefully into a chair, then filling her cup. "So, what are you doing in our country, señor?"

He paused between bites and pinned her with a long stare over the rim of his coffee cup, soaking up her beauty, his eyes lingering longer than they should and liking what he saw.

"I'm looking for a fellow," he said in a struggled whisper that caused one to listen hard just to hear the words. "Maybe you can help me. He's a big man, big as me. He'd have frosty gray hair and a scar along his left cheek. Here." he said, tracing a finger slowly along his cheek. "Likely goes by the name of Colonel Mattox. Ever hear tell of a man like that?"

"Si, señor, there is such a man. His hacienda lies a day's ride toward the setting sun where the San Miguel River flows through the Sierra Madre Mountains. It is a great hacienda, one of the finest in all of Mexico.

This man, is he a friend of yours, señor?"

Shiloh didn't answer for a long space of time. He stared at his coffee cup. His pale green eyes squinted to narrow slits and he felt hatred cloud his whiskered face.

"Not likely," he said from behind clenched teeth. "I'm going to kill him."

He watched her face as he said it, waiting for the shock of the words.

There was no shock, no surprise, no reaction at all. This was no naive young girl, he decided.

"The man you seek, señor, he is a very bad man. Many bandidos ride for him. It is said he sends them across the Rio Grande into your country on raids. They steal herds of cattle, rob, and plunder, then flee back across the border, knowing the Americano soldaderas cannot follow. They are led by a pistolero called El lobo, which means, the wolf. He is a killer. Some of his men were here only a few days ago.

"They were here?" Shiloh asked, interest creeping into his voice. "What did they want?"

"The water, of course," Consuela replied, not at all concerned. "Like all the others, they come for the water."

"Others?" he whispered. "What others?"

"The Apaches, the Comanchero, the bandidos, they all come to drink the water from God's well, señor."

"You saying they come and drink the water and don't bother you folks?" he asked, finding the story hard to believe.

"Si, señor, it has been so for many years."

He thought on that for a spell, shaking his head, completely puzzled.

Whoever heard of such a thing? Still giving the story thoughtful consideration, he absently raked the last bite from his plate and transported it to his mouth. Draining his coffee cup, he fished two dollars from his pocket and dropped it on the table. Pushing back, he unlimbered to his full height.

"Enjoyed the meal and the company," he told her, clamping the worn out old Confederate hat on his sand colored hair that needed a cutting. "Maybe I'll ride this way again."

He picked up the small sack of food the man had prepared and strode to the open door. From long habit he paused. His gaze swept to and fro before stepping outside. Taking up Buck's reins, he led him down to the well.

Again and again he filled the watering trough for his horse. He felt eyes upon him. He swept a gaze around. It was the girl. She stood by the door of the little cantina, her back against the wall, one foot drawn up behind her. Her eyes bore pleasing holes in him. He returned her gaze for a long minute, then tore his eyes away and set in filling his four canteens.

He was about to cap off the last one when the padre walked up. As stifling hot as it was, he wore a black robe from his neck to just above his sandal clad feet. A white collar, turned around backwards, ringed his neck. A little black topcap sat on snow-white, collar length hair. The pleasant smile on his face looked real and unforced.

Shiloh's sweeping gaze briefly touched the man's eyes and froze. They were like no eyes he had ever seen. Haunting, glassy looking eyes that stared straight ahead, looking but not seeing. The old priest was blind.

"Good day to you, my son," the holy man said in a soft, pleasant voice. "You are a weary traveler I perceive."

"Yes, sir. My name's Shiloh. You're the one that dug the well, I hear."

"I was only an instrument in the hands of God," the holy man said. "We all are, you know."

"Maybe you, padre," Shiloh whispered in a gravelly voice, looping his canteens over his saddle horn. "I doubt your God would call me that."

"Do you not believe in God, my son?"

"I believe in this," Shiloh said, patting his tied down Colt. "Don't reckon I ever saw God, or a miracle either for that matter."

"One does not have to see a miracle to enjoy the benefits from it," the padre said. "Sometimes a miracle, like God himself, is better seen with the heart, than with the eyes. Where will your journey take you, my son?"

"Likely to hell," Shiloh said, matter-of-factly, "but not before I've settled some old scores."

"I hear much hate in your heart, traveler."

"Yeah," Shiloh whispered bitterly. "Well, I got a lot of reason to hate."

"Hate is a beast that devours the soul, my son."

Shiloh allowed that last statement to slide into his mind and settle for a spell before replying.

"Tell me something, padre," Shiloh asked, feeling a questioning furrow crease his forehead. Leather creaked as he toed a stirrup and lifted a leg over his saddle, settling against the cantle. "Why do you reckon all these bloodthirsty killers never bother you folks when they ride in and drink the water from your well? Never heard of a thing like that."

"El Aqua Dios is for all of God's children, my son," the aged priest said. "It is a sanctuary. A safe haven for all who thirst, either of the body or of the soul."

"I reckon I'm just looking for something to help me understand what I don't understand," Shiloh said, lifting the reins and kneeing his buckskin.

"Adios, padre."

"Vaya con Dios, traveler," the holy man said. "We shall meet again, I think."

Shiloh pointed the big geldings nose into the vanishing sun and heeled him into a high hoofing canter. There was a man over yonder that needed killing. He'd best get at it.

Twisting in his saddle, he peered back to see both the priest and the girl standing side by side near the well, staring after him. With a swipe of her hand she brushed long strands of dark hair from her face, pushed there by the wind, then lifted a hand in good-bye. She shore made a picture for a man to tuck away in his mind.

A brilliant red sunball approached the distant line of hazy-blue mountains slowly, timidly, like a lover about to say a final good-bye. It gently kissed the lofty peaks one last time before dying for the day and being buried somewhere in the depth of the western horizon.

Behind it, in one last hurrah, in a final legacy, it splashed the velvety blue sky ablaze with shades of boiling reds, yellows, oranges, and golds, and could have come only from God's own paintbrush. Streaks of light shot across the sky as if from a great unseen cannon, careened off the few puffy white clouds, framing them in shiny silver.

Shiloh settled in his saddle. Hypnotized by the ever changing panorama flashing before his eyes, the rhythmic crunching of his horse's hooves, and the singsong creak of saddle leather, all played a tune to soothe a man's soul.

He was tired. It had been near four months since he left Sweetwater, most of that time spent in the saddle. He felt shock at the thought. Four months?

He hadn't thought of it in terms of months before. It had piled up in little pieces, one day at a time, one more lead to follow up, one more bit of information, and usually, one more dead end. Maybe this time he had found the Colonel, maybe now it would end.

The distant call of a coyote broke into his thoughts. Dusky darkness rolled across the desert and settled like a dense fog. Gnarled mesquite bushes, catclaws, and tall prickly pear cast eerie shadows across the rolling sand dunes.

As darkness swallowed the last hint of light, the seemingly uninhabited land came alive, teeming with life. Desert scorpions emerged from crevices and holes and scampered about, their deadly tails arched over their backs, seeking an easy prey. A night owl called, a coyote yelped, and Shiloh rode on into the night.

Something spooked the big buckskin causing him to suddenly shy sideways. Instinctively, in a lightning blur of motion, a Colt was clutched in Shiloh's hand, the hammer eared back, its deathly nose seeking the source of alarm.

A desert sidewinder slithered sideways beneath a clump of sagebrush, coiled itself into a tight loop, its ugly head raised threateningly. Shiloh lowered the hammer and returned the weapon to its holster. His nightly ritual of practicing at least an hour had paid off. He could tell he was much faster than he had been only a few months before.

Guided by the stars and aided by a three-quarter moon, he rode on through the night. Just before first light he found a deep arroyo and reined down into it. He was dead tired. He had ridden from sunup till sunup. He would rest during the day and travel only at night, well aware that, in the desert, any movement sends a telltale dust signal that can be seen for miles.

Both he and the buckskin would have to make do with a dry camp. If all went well, he figured they should make the river sometime the next night. Consuela had said it was only a day's ride. Consuela . . .now that was a pleasurable thought. He drew her memory from his mind and warmed his heart with it.

A quick pull of pigging strings freed his bedroll. He found a smooth place, rolled it out, and propped his saddle at one end for a pillow.

Laying his Stevens sawed off double barrel shotgun beside his bedroll and worming contours for comfort into the soft sand, he stretched out his full length, propped both hands behind his head, and stared at the stars until they melted away into the velvety darkness of exhausted sleep.

The sweltering heat from a boiling hot sun woke him. He shielded his eyes and squinted, judging it to be near two hours past noon. Rising, he moved his bedroll under the partial shade of some scrawny mesquite bushes, stretched and scratched his sand colored hair.

It was pitiful little, but he fed Buck what was left of the oats from the small sack tied behind his saddle, then poured two canteens of water into his cavalry hat and held it so he could sip it dry.

"You'll have to make do with that till we can get to the river tonight," he told his buckskin, talking to him like he would a friend.

He untied the little grub sack Consuela's father had fixed for him and peeked inside. To his delight, he found two pieces of barbecued goat, a half dozen hard boiled eggs, and a stack of corn tortillas. He ate half of everything, resisted the temptation to eat the other half, and washed it down with half a canteen of water.

Laying back down on his bedroll, his mind drifted back to something the old padre said. "Hate is a beast that devours the soul." He considered that a spell and reckoned the holy man was right. Ever since the hanging, it had been gnawing at his insides, eating away at him. He had to get it settled.

Shadows lengthened. The sun arched downward toward the line of high mountains forming the western horizon. He rose, saddled and cinched his gelding, and swung into leather.

"Let's make tracks, big fellow," he told his buckskin. "There's a whole river full of water waiting over yonder for us."

The first blush of dawn found horse and rider standing belly deep in the cool, swift running San Miguel River. The rugged Sierra Madre Mountain range loomed ominously over the fertile, green river valley. It's lofty peaks punching holes in the clouds. Just below where they sat, the river rushed into a canyon-like opening, cut through solid rock by centuries past. The distant roar of a waterfall somewhere in the bowels of the canyon reached his hearing.

Sitting his saddle, Shiloh peered through the grayness of first light and slowly scanned the countryside. Off in the distance, upriver and to his left, he could make out the vague outline of a large, walled compound. It was nestled on a flat plateau overlooking the river. It stood like a fort butted up against a sheer cliff that rose three hundred feet straight up.

That would be the walled hacienda Consuela had told him about, the Colonel's house.

As dawn gave birth to light, his searching gaze climbed along the mountainside that served as a backdrop for the compound. Pine and scrub cedar clung precariously to it's steep slopes. The few swags he saw were rendered impassable by fields of rock, broken off from the cliffs above.

On the very top, he spotted a rock bluff that would serve as a perfect lookout point. Getting up to it was another matter. He could see no possible way even a man could get up there, let alone a horse and rider.

Acting partly on a hunch, partly on experience from his growing up years hunting in the Smoky Mountains near his home, but mostly out of desperation, he turned the buckskin's nose into the canyon.

Urging the reluctant gelding into the steep-walled opening, they waded slowly along the rushing stream. They splashed along for the most part of a quarter-mile. The deafening roar of the waterfall grew louder, drowning out all other sound. He was getting too close. He had to turn back. He twisted in the saddle, ready to give up and turn back. That's when he saw it.

The hundred foot wall of solid rock had cracked sometime in times past and left a cutback crevice. It angled back so sharply it would go unnoticed by anyone coming downstream. He himself had passed within a few feet without being aware of its presence.

Turning his horse, he splashed over to examine the crevice closer. It was a narrow crack that climbed steeply up the side of the mountain at a sharp angle. Hundreds, perhaps thousands of years had filled the bottom of the crack with a thick layer of soil. In the soft ground he could see older tracks of both deer and elk.

It was clear they used the crevice to come down from the mountaintop to drink from the river but it had been awhile.. That told him it was unlikely there was an easier way off the mountain or they would use it. It was also obvious they had found an easier source of water.

If an elk, with their huge racks, could make it through the tight opening, just maybe he could too. Swinging from the saddle into waist deep water, he climbed into the crevice. Tugging on Buck's reins, he urged the buckskin up out of the water into the opening. The gelding's powerful hindquarter muscles bulged as he surged up into the crack at the urging of his master.

Shiloh leaned sharply forward and started the climb up the steep path, tugging the long reins after him. The buckskin lunged upward, leap by leap, climbing higher with each jump. Its front hooves digging deep, pulling, its back hooves planting, then propelling its weight forward a few feet at a time.

A terrible thought struck Shiloh's mind. What if those tracks were older because something had blocked the crevice somewhere above? How would they get back down? He should have thought about that before, it was too late to turn back now.

On and on they struggled. The buckskin labored gamely as it fought the slope. Muscles bulged. Its sides heaved. Great blasts of air made sucking sounds through the horse's nose. Blood vessels in the horse's neck stood out as if about to burst and still the loyal horse lunged onward and upward.

Shiloh's own sides heaved. His leg muscles ached. His mouth opened wide as he fought to draw air into his starving lungs with labored gasps. He knew that if they stopped they would never be able to start again. He climbed on.

Finally they broke clear, emerging from the crevice onto a small plateau. He collapsed onto the ground for a spell. Buck stood on shaky legs, his head down. His sweat-soaked body gleamed in the sun's early light.

"You done good, big fellow," he said in his raspy voice, reaching to pat the big horse on its neck. "You done real good."

Pushing to his knees, then to his feet, he walked over to the edge of the rock facing and peered down to the river far below. Downstream a ways, the water seemed to drop off the edge of the earth. The roar of the waterfall was deafening.

Swinging his gaze around and upward, he saw a rock field that seemed impassable. The jumbled mass of house sized boulders blocked their way from climbing farther up the steep sloped mountainside. Now what? Had they made that climb for nothing?

Squatting, he examined the ground closely. A faint game trail led directly into the field of rocks. Taking up the buckskin's reins, he set out afoot, leading his horse. The trail twisted and turned, weaving its way through the rocks, climbing steadily upward. Breaking free of the rocks, he found himself facing a solid stand of scrub cedar.

The ground was hard, mostly solid rock. He had to search to find where the trail entered the dense growth of cedars. Finally he found it, and led his horse higher along the weaving trail.

Suddenly he broke clear of the thicket and passed between two huge boulders into the prettiest little valley one could ever imagine. It was no more than fifty yards across and carpeted with lush green grass. Several large pine trees shaded a small rock tank that lay along one side of the valley. It was filled with fresh water. That explained why the animals tracks were older, he thought. They too had found this temporary water source.

Dropping Buck's reins so he could munch the grass, Shiloh moved past a huge pine tree to the edge of the cliff. Peering down, he could look right into the Colonel's compound far below.

"This will do just fine," he said out loud to himself.

Retracing his steps, he stripped his horse of saddle and bridle allowing it freedom to graze its fill. Hefting his saddle over his shoulder with one hand, he carried it and dropped it in the shade of the big pine. Digging around in his saddlebags, he found his cavalry issued field glass and bellied down on the flat rock at the edge of the cliff. Bringing the glass to eye, he carefully studied the entire area below.

It was quite an impressive layout the Colonel had. Situated on a flat, grassy plateau, dotted with large pines, and overlooking the river below, it was a beautiful spot sure enough. Built like a fort with ten foot high adobe walls surrounding the enclosure on three sides, it butted up against the sheer rock wall of the mountain along the back.

He counted three openings in the wall. The front gate had heavy double doors that opened toward the river. A smaller opening in each side wall also had strong looking doors.

Inside the compound itself, Shiloh counted four buildings. The impressive main house was a flat roofed, adobe structure with large peeled roof poles protruding along the top. It dominated one whole corner of the compound. Flowering azalea bushes lined red tile walkways that wound through a well cared for garden. Hanging baskets swung from a pole arbor that shaded a red tile patio along the entire front of the hacienda. One could easily see a woman's touch about the place.

Near the back of the compound, he identified a stable that opened into a pole corral. Six beautiful horses milled about, one of which was the most magnificent white stallion he had ever seen.

Scanning the field glass along the river, he spotted a cluster of adobe shanties with a large corral nearby. Most likely the Colonel's workers, or the bandidos Consuela had mentioned, lived there. Scattered all along the river valley, a large herd of cattle grazed peacefully.

The fresh mountain air washed over him like a cool mountain stream. His lungs drew in the sweet scent of pine. This was a nice place, he thought, lying back and listening to the breeze whispering through the pines. An image of Consuela emerged in his mind.

He remembered her beautiful face and the crinkled corners of an easy smile. The memory brought a powerful longing to see her again. He had never met anyone like her. There was no illusion about her in his mind, he knew she was no innocent young girl. She seemed so self-assured, so in control. Her tantalizing beauty haunted him

Taking up one of his canteens, he tilted it to his lips and tasted the sweetness of the water from, what Consuela called God's well. His mind wandered back to the little village of El Aqua Dios.

It was a strange place. Its mysterious well that shouldn't be there. What was there about the place that kept sworn enemies from killing each other on sight? What strange power? What mystical belief prevented bloodthirsty Indians from murdering the townspeople?

The blind old padre's words kept rolling around in his mind. Over and over he could hear him saying, "hate is a beast that devours the soul." It was true. He was a walking testimony. His very soul was consumed with hatred for the Colonel. Could anyone blame him?

As the tangled events of the day of his hanging boiled up from his memory and flooded his mind for the ten thousandth time, all other thoughts were swept aside like so many tiny twigs before a raging torrent. He broke into a cold sweat. A gloved hand lifted. Fingers pushed aside the faded neckerchief and traced the ugly scar around his neck left there by the noose.

CHAPTER IX

Colonel Sam Mattox sat at the end of a long mahogany dining table in an elaborately furnished room. One finger curled around a fat cigar and brought it casually to his lips. Dark eyes peered through blue tendrils of smoke at the six men gathered around the table. They gazed attentively back at him, waiting for him to speak. His other hand toyed with a brown envelope lying on the table in front of him.

"Mr. Duncan," the Colonel said, sweeping his eyes around the table and allowing them to come to rest on a tall, wide shouldered man with a full beard. In the army, he had served under Colonel Mattox for a year before deserting. "You've just returned from an excursion up into Arizona. Would you give us your report?"

"Well," Ben Duncan said, glancing around the table. "We had information that a large shipment of silver would be moving from the mines around Silver City on its way to the mint in Denver. We took twenty men and ambushed the wagons. We killed the guards and drivers and made it back safe with the whole shipment."

"Excellent," Mattox said. "Where do you suppose we got the information about the shipment?"

"I reckon in one of those envelopes like that one there," the man said.

"Mr. Folsom," the colonel said, fixing his eyes on a tall, slim fellow with a pockmarked face and cold eyes. "I saw your men drive in a herd of fine looking cattle a few days ago. Tell us how you come by them."

"My men raided a ranch up near Casa Grande. We wiped out the owner and his family and all the hands. There weren't nobody left to give us trouble so we just rounded them up and drove 'em back."

"How did we know about that particular ranch and its cattle?"

"From whoever sends you those envelopes, I reckon," the man said.

"Exactly. My friend, which we all know only as Mr. X, sends information by a courier to El Paso at a prearranged time and place each month. Our own Mr. Wilkins's job is to meet him and bring the sealed envelope back here to me. Mr. X always seals the envelope with hot wax and places the imprint of his ring in the wax to insure the information is seen only by me. Is that not correct, Mr. Wilkins?"

"Yes, sir," the frightened man breathed.

"How long have you served with me, Mr. Wilkins?"

"Uh...going on three years now," he replied, his voice breaking.

The Colonel's cold stare fixed on a smallish fellow with nervous eyes. The man was clearly scared. He was sweating profusely. His eyes darted from one to the other around the table. Without another word the colonel pushed back his chair and rose. He strode casually around the table to stand directly behind the man named Wilkins.

"Unfortunately," Mattox said, his voice taking on a cold, hard, tone.

"The envelope I just received had been opened, hadn't it, Mr. Wilkins?"

"I-I can explain," the man stammered. "It was open when the other courier gave it to me."

"Then you should have sent it back to Mr. X and let him deal with his own courier, just as I must deal with you."

The Colonel withdrew a pistol from his flapped holster. The sound of its hammer being drawn back sounded like a clap of thunder in the quiet of the room as the nose of the pistol touched the back of the man's head. The Colonel squeezed the trigger.

The blast was deafening. The man's head exploded like a ripe watermelon, sending blood and bone and brain fragments flying across the mahogany table, splattering the other five men around it. Chairs overturned. Men leaped to their feet, wiping great drops of blood from their faces.

"Sit down!" the Colonel shouted the order. "No one has been dismissed."

Calmly...almost casually, he replaced the pistol and returned to his chair. He sat down, drew a long inhale from his cigar, and swept a slow gaze over the faces of the remaining four men as they took their seats.

They were hard men, men that had no scruples, men that would kill their own mother in a heartbeat if he ordered them to do so. That was the kind of men he had to have riding for him.

"You're all paid rather handsomely. I will not tolerate disobedience. You have just witnessed the penalty for disobeying orders," he exhaled a cloud of blue smoke. "Mr. X sent information about an army payroll that would have netted us a very large profit. Unfortunately, it would be too dangerous now to act on the information since it may well have been compromised. It could be a trap. Instead, we'll execute the bank robbery in Hobbs, New Mexico, we've been rehearsing. Mr. Carter, you will lead the raid. Take twenty men. You will leave in two days. El lobo, have you been able to recruit more riders for us. We need another dozen men at least."

"I have a dozen good men waiting for me in Chihuahua," the pistolero assured him.

"Excellent. Very well then, you're all dismissed. Have two of the guards remove Mr. Wilkins, and tell one of the house girls to clean up this mess."

Rising, the Colonel turned on his heels and marched from the room. He strode to a large living room near the front of the hacienda where Romana Diego waited.

As it did each time he looked upon her, her beauty took his breath away. She stood as he entered the room. Her jet black hair framed flawless, walnut colored skin. Dark, sparkling eyes swung to gaze appreciatively at him as her full lips lifted in a smile. He extended a crooked arm.

"Walk with me in the garden," he invited, his voice becoming soft and attentive.

Reaching a hand, she threaded his elbow and moved gracefully beside him. Together they strolled along the flower edged tile path that wound its way toward a shaded fountain fed by a mountain spring.

"I heard a shot," she stated.

"It was nothing to concern you," he dismissed the query. "I have a surprise for you."

Withdrawing a small, velvet covered box from his pocket, he snapped it open and held it out before her. The large, diamond earrings caught the late afternoon sun and sent rainbows of color shooting out in every direction. A gasp of air caught in her throat. Her dark eyes rounded. A hand flew to her open lips.

"Oh, Sam," she exclaimed, leaning to plant a lingering kiss on his cheek. "They are beautiful."

"They ought to be," he said, pleased with her reaction. "They cost me a small fortune."

"You will be well repaid," she purred seductively, offering a tantalizing suggestion of things to come.

Sam Mattox had no doubt about the truthfulness of her promise. These past few months with her had been far beyond his wildest dreams. Her tears dried quickly after he and his men had killed Don Diego, her late husband, and laid claim, not only to his magnificent hacienda, but also to his wife.

Shiloh awoke with a start from his familiar haunting nightmare. He had dozed off. The marching dead men had followed him here to the mountaintop. Sleeving cold sweat from his face and shaking his head to clear his mind, he jerked the brass field glass to his eye and saw him. Colonel Mattox emerged from the hacienda with a beautiful señorita on his arm.

She was dressed in black riding pants and a white blouse. Her long black hair was gathered in the back and tied with a white ribbon. She strolled beside the Colonel with an easy, confident stride. They stopped beside a fountain.

Time hadn't changed his sworn enemy. Tall. Powerful. Square shouldered. He walked beside the señorita along the walkway with the air of an aristocra, the very picture of authority.

An ocean of hatred washed over Shiloh. His hand snatched the .52 caliber Sharps long rifle from its saddle boot. Methodically, he withdrew a big shell from the ammunition belt, shoved it into the chamber, slammed it closed, and jammed the big buffalo gun to his shoulder. His right eye sighted down the long barrel and laid the front sight squarely on the Colonel's big chest.

His jaws clamped shut. Teeth ground. He sucked in a great draught of air, then let it out in a slow slide of breath that made a rattling sound. One light touch of his finger and it would all be over.

No! That would be too quick, too easy. He must die by the bayonet, just like the ones he had forced Shiloh to kill. The Colonel must feel the bite of cold steel. He must know it was coming. Shiloh wanted the man to feel the hot sweat of fear before he died.

From the corner of his eye, Shiloh caught a movement off to his right.

He lowered the Sharps and peered through his field glass. Several men emerged from a side door of the house. They moved quickly toward the corral and waiting, saddled horses. There were four of them, all tough looking Americans. They mounted and rode out of the compound at a gallop through the open front gate.

Others appeared. Two Mexicans carried the body of an American. Even from that distance, Shiloh could see most of the man's head was missing. Another tall Mexican followed, sauntered to the corral, mounted a big, rawboned sorrel, and kicked it into a short lope toward the adobe shanties upstream.

The sun slid behind the mountain. Twilight spread its shadowy cloak of grayness over the Sierra Madre Mountains. Darkness waited impatiently to claim the land.

Shiloh led his buckskin back down the mountain. He used a branch from a scrub cedar to brush out his tracks at the entrance to the crevice. He wanted to keep this place his own secret. It might come in handy again.

Riding upstream, he emerged from the mouth of the canyon. Peering through the moonlight, he swept the countryside with a searching gaze. Seeing no movement, he urged his horse up the middle of the river to a spot even with the front gate of the compound.

Twisting in the saddle, he loosed pigging strings and fetched the leather bundle from behind his saddle. Carefully unrolling it, he stared for a long moment at the six sewn pockets of the leather pouch as one would look into the coffin of a departed loved one. Each compartment contained a bayonet. Each bayonet had taken the life of a fellow Confederate prisoner of war. He wore the seventh in a scabbard on his belt.

Carefully, almost reverently, he selected one and withdrew

it from its resting place. Its shiny blade caught light from the moon and flashed off into the night, as if signaling its awakening.

Rolling the pouch back up, he retied it behind his saddle. From his saddlebag, he withdrew a short rope that had been fashioned into a noose, the same noose with which he had been hanged those many months ago. His lips compressed to a tight slit and the skin on his neck crawled as he felt the familiar rope.

With the bayonet and rope in one hand, and the cedar branch in the other, he stepped from his saddle into knee-deep water. Leaving the buckskin ground hitched in the middle of the river, he waded to the bank and climbed the sloping hillside to the closed gate.

Shiloh glanced down at the bayonet in his hand. For a fleeting moment it appeared a thing of beauty. Its shiny, razor sharp surface gleamed in the moonlight, disguising its only purpose for existence, to kill. In his own hand, this weapon had been used to snuff out the life of one of his fellow prisoners. Now it would be used to send a message, a message of impending death.

His arm swung. The needlepoint plunged deep into the heavy wood of the double gate. With his other hand he hung the looped hangman's noose over the protruding bayonet. There would be no doubt about its meaning. The Colonel would know. Shiloh wanted the Colonel to sweat for awhile before he killed him.

Backing down the slope toward the river, Shiloh used the cedar branch to brush out his tracks. Toeing a stirrup, he swung into leather and splashed back downstream. Exiting the river onto a rocky surface, then onto a heavy cushion of grass, he pointed the buckskin toward the little village of El Agua Dios.

The morning sun hung two hours high when he rode into the tiny village and reined up in front of the well. An older woman in a faded white shift paused to stare, then returned to her task of hanging wet clothes across a line stretched between two buildings. Chickens scratched and pecked in the sand. A small boy, looking to be maybe four or five cast a look his way, smiled happily, and disappeared around the corner of the building with a wooden bucket in one hand and leading a goat with a heavy bag of milk.

Shiloh's gaze strayed toward the cantina as he drew from the well. He slaked his own thirst and began filling his four canteens while the buckskin drank thirstily from the brimming water trough. Consuela paused for a moment when she stepped through the door of the cantina and saw him, then came toward him with hurried steps. A happy smile lit her face and told him what he wanted to know.

"Buenas dias, señorita," he greeted, lifting a gloved thumb and finger to the brim of his hat. "You look mighty perky this morning."

"Perky?" she laughed, sashaying up with her hands clasped behind her back and a questioning look showing on her pretty face. "That is a word I do not know."

"Perky," he repeated. "It means...well...it means happy and pretty at the same time."

A smile graced her face and pushed away the questioning look. She leaned her back against the parapet of the well and watched as he resumed filling his canteens.

"I was hoping you would come again," she offered, dropping her eyes to the sand, then lifting them to find his with a lingering gaze. "But I was afraid you wouldn't."

"I said I might," his raspy voice said simply.

"Did you?"

"Not yet," he said, understanding her unasked question.

"I was worried about you," she said, watching her sandal toe a mark in the sand.

He paused from his task and engaged her with a lingering gaze. Their eyes met. Her long look didn't waver. Was he seeing something in those dark, sparkling eyes that wasn't there?

"I had to come back to get some supplies," he said, clearing his dry throat.

"Was that the only reason?" she asked, as she pursed her lips in a mocking pout.

"I was kind of hoping I might see you again, too," he admitted.

"I said a prayer for you," she said, suddenly sounding serious and drifting a hand to touch his arm and allowing it to linger. "You look hungry. I will make you a morning meal."

"You shore won't get no argument out of me about that," he told her, feeling the touch of her hand on his arm and wishing it would never go away. "I'll come on up to the cantina when I'm finished."

She turned. He stood transfixed. His eyes followed every movement as she walked toward the cantina. She moved with her head held high. Her easy, measured steps accented the gentle swaying of her body under the loose skirt.

For a long minute he stared. It was like he was caught in a whirlpool, being drawn deeper and deeper under her spell. He had never known anyone like her. She was the most desirable woman he had ever encountered.

As if she had heard his thoughts, her head twisted to cast a lingering look and a tantalizing smile over her shoulder. Embarrassed, he quickly tore his gaze away, afraid she might read his thinking through his eyes.

Capping off the last of his canteens, he flicked a look at the little trading post. He needed some supplies. Taking up Buck's reins, he headed that way.

"Buenas dias, señor," the friendly little Mexican fellow greeted as Shiloh pushed through the open door of the jumbled little shop.

"Buenas dias," Shiloh replied. "¿Habla ud. ingles."

"Si, señor," the man smiled broadly. "The padre teach all of us in the village to speak your language."

"I'm needing some trail supplies, mind if I look around a bit?"

"Oh, no, señor," the shop owner said happily. "I will be happy to help you."

The place was small and the usable supplies were sparse. Shiloh settled for a sack of dried jerky, a tin of coffee, a sack of black beans, and some dried fruit. He added a sack of feed for the buckskin. He decided he'd lay in a stack of tortillas from Consuela's father at the cantina. He paid the man and headed up the sloping hillside toward the cantina.

His nose trailed the sweet aroma of hot coffee and found a pot and two empty cups waiting for him on the only table wiped clean of the ever present dust. He lifted out a chair and settled into it.

By the time he drained his second cup, Consuela emerged from the back room carrying a plateful of scrambled eggs mixed liberally with red peppers. A second plate was stacked high with corn tortillas.

"I'd be pleased if you'd join me," Shiloh told her.

That happy little smile that made him warm inside creased her lips and she scooted out a chair. She refilled his cup, poured one for herself, and watched silently as he dug into the food like a starving wolf pup. He made short work of cleaning his plate, then sat back and sipped his coffee. A satisfied look occupied his face.

"Do you have a man?" he asked pointedly, pinning her dark eyes with a searching look.

"I was married," she said, dropping her eyes to stare at her coffee cup. My husband was killed four months ago. I have a son. His name is Benito. He is four years old."

"How was your husband killed?"

"He was a vaquero for señor Don Diego at the great hacienda. The Americano colonel you seek, he and his men killed señor Diego and all those that worked for him. My husband was one of them. They took over the hacienda as their own. It is said the Colonel also took señora Diego as his woman. You asked if I had a man. I do not. The pistolero called El Lobo wants me for his woman."

"What do you want?" he asked, probing her eyes with his own.

"I hate him!" she spat the words out like they tasted bad. "I would kill myself before I let him touch me."

"Where is your son?" he asked. "I would like to meet him."

"He stays with my father's sister while I help in the cantina. My mother died when I was very young."

They talked, and sipped their coffee. Consuela told him of her life here in the tiny village. She talked of a life of hardship and poverty. Mostly though, she talked of Benito. Shiloh saw how her eyes lit up when she spoke of her son.

"I want something more for my son, señor. I wish for him a better life than he could have here in El Aqua Dios. Here, he is either a goat herder or a bandidos. There is no other choice."

He liked being with her. They visited with her father and walked down to her aunt's casa together. She was the woman he had seen earlier hanging out a washing. As it turned out, Benito was the happy little boy that had smiled at him that morning.

Shiloh immediately took a liking to the energetic young boy. He swung the boy up into the saddle and led the buckskin around the village.

"Mama," the boy called happily, "Look at me."

"Si," she laughed and called back, "I see you."

Late in the day Consuela and Shiloh strolled together to the top of the hill behind the mission. They sat on the sandy hilltop and watched the lowering sun slide toward the distant horizon. Their eyes met. Their hands touched. Their hearts joined. A lump climbed into his throat. The bell in the mission tower sounded.

"What does it mean?" he asked.

"It is time for evening mass," she explained. "Would you come with me?"

They rose and made their way slowly down the hill toward the mission. From all over the tiny village people were doing the same. Silently, reverently, they filed into the small building. He walked beside Consuela as they entered.

She paused, knelt slightly, and crossed herself before they slipped into the last of five wooden benches. This was all strange to him. It was nothing like the little church back in Sweetwater, Tennessee.

Across the front of the room was a platform. At the back of it, built into a recess, stood a statue of a pretty lady holding a tiny baby in her arms. The statue was beautiful. Its presence dominated the whole room. Underneath the statue, on a table covered with a white covering, stood a foot high gold cross.

Shiloh stared at it, disbelieving his eyes. Unless he missed his guess, that cross was made of pure gold. Its polished surface caught up the flickering light from a dozen candles and sent reflections bouncing around the room, as if the cross had a life of its own. As Shiloh stared, transfixed, at the cross, he sensed, rather than saw, Consuela move silently from beside him. She made her way toward the front where a small railing separated the platform from the worshipers.

Little candles stood as bright pinpoints, some of them shining red where they had burned down in their ruby colored glasses. He watched as she took a long match and lit one, then knelt to one knee and bowed her head in a brief prayer. She rose, crossed herself reverently, then returned to stand beside him. Others followed her example.

When it was over, they strolled silently back to the cantina. Señor Cordona, Consuela's father, served them a delicious supper, then retired behind the bar to busy himself cleaning glasses.

They had finished eating and were lingering over a sipping cup when the sound of horses reining up reached his ears. Consuela heard it too. A sudden look of panic swept across her beautiful face.

"It is them, señor," she said frantically. "You must run out the back door. They will kill you!"

"I ain't much on running," he said in a whispered voice.

His right hand flicked the traveling thong off the bone handled

Colt on his right hip. His left hand snaked underneath the tattered serape to it's twin in the belly holster and rested there.

"Don't worry. It'll be all right."

The riders were guffawing and shouting to one another as they dismounted and pushed through the open front door. There were five of them. All tough looking Mexicans. Pistoleros. Four wore bandoleers that crisscrossed their chests. Straw sombreros partially shaded their whiskered faces. It was the fifth man, the one in front, that captured Shiloh's attention.

Shiloh didn't have to wonder who he was. Tall. Thin. Near gaunt looking. Wide in the shoulders. Narrow of hip. His arms appeared too long for his body.

A black, flat brimmed hat with a snakeskin band hung suspended down his back by a neck cord. His face looked like dried, cracked leather, obviously cooked that way by too many years in the blistering sun. A cruel looking slash of mouth had a nervous twitch in one corner.

The man's eyes swept the room and came to rest on Shiloh and the girl.

He stopped. His gaze locked upon Shiloh. The eyes, they were cold, menacing. They were the eyes of a wolf. This was the one Consuela had called El Lobo—he was well named.

All five newcomers stood unmoving for a long minute. Shiloh returned the wolf-eyed stare, each man appraising the other. Shiloh's hidden left hand tightened its grip on the Colt and slowly slid it from its belly holster, thumbing back the hammer to full cock.

A look of anger swept across El Lobo's face. Without a word he strode the few steps to their table. His long left arm shot out and a hand grasped Consuela's arm, jerking her from the chair. Wheeling, the Mexican pistolero headed for the door, half dragging the screaming girl behind him.

Sitting down his cup, Shiloh pushed back from the table and stretched to his full height before speaking. "Let the girl go," the raspy, whispered words squeezed out.

El Lobo stopped. For a brief space of time he stood motionless, then violently flung the girl from him into a nearby table. Slowly he turned. As he did his four compadres slid sideways to either side, creating a wider target.

"She's my woman," the man snarled wickedly.

"I reckon that's for her to decide, not you," Shiloh whispered, keeping all five in his vision.

"I'm not your woman!" Consuela screamed at him, anger mixing with terror in her voice. "I will never be your woman."

A quick step and he stood before her. One of those long arms drew back. The backhanded swipe split her lips. Blood splayed in flying droplets as she sprawled onto the floor.

Shiloh felt a deep furrow plow across his forehead. His pale green eyes squinted to narrow slits. A flash of sudden anger burned white-hot in his belly. His jaw set. Teeth gnashed together and jaw muscles bulged as he spoke the whispered words.

"You ever touch her again, I'll kill you." It was a statement as certain as the sun rising in the east.

The pistolero turned slowly to face Shiloh. The large rowels on his Mexican spurs made a soft jingling sound in the deathly quietness of the room as his legs spread apart in a gunfighter's stance. Curled fingers waited barely an inch from the pearl handled pistols on either hip. Wolfish eyes flashed hatred and swept Shiloh from head to toe, then back again.

"In case you hadn't noticed," El Lobo sneered confidently, "there's five of us. We'll kill you, sure."

A slight smile crooked Shiloh's lips. His cold gaze locked on the dark wolf eyes.

"Maybe so. Then again, maybe not," he whispered. "Either way, you'll be the first to die."

Seconds ticked by, each seeming an eternity. No one moved. No one breathed. The room was as quiet as a graveyard at midnight with each knowing the next heartbeat might well be their last.

Another presence filled the room. Its shadow stepped between the combatants. It was the old blind padre.

"There will be no killing in El Aqua Dios," he stated simply. "Is there a shortage of land outside this sanctuary for such evil things? Go!" he ordered, raising an arm to point to the door. "God is not pleased with your presence."

The pistoleros hesitated for only an instant. Then, without a word or backwards glance, they turned on their heels and stomped out the door. All except one. At the door El Lobo paused and turned.

"Who are you?" he asked, fighting back the anger in his shaking voice.

"The name's Shiloh."

"You are a dead man, gringo. A dead man." the pistolero snarled, before turning and stalking out the door after his men.

"Tell your boss I'm coming for him," Shiloh called after him. "Anyone gets in the way, they'll die too."

Shiloh rushed to Consuela's side. Her father was there, wiping blood and tears from her face with a clean cloth. Outside, the sound of retreating horses was interrupted by a piercing scream that split the night. Shiloh rushed to the door in time to see El Lobo boot a stirrup and climb onto a black and white pinto. Under one arm he held a kicking and screaming little boy. It was Benito. Consuela's aunt lay in a heap, filling the night with frantic pleadings.

The bandidos jammed spurs to their horse's flanks and pounded out of the tiny village and were swallowed up by the darkness.

"See to your sister," Shiloh rasped loudly over his shoulder as he broke into a run.

The buckskin stood tethered at a hitching rail in front of the cantina. He reached the big gelding and leaped into the saddle. Wheeling his horse, he lifted it into a belly-to-the-ground run after the fleeing kidnappers.

According to what the old padre had told him earlier, the one called El Lobo had done the unthinkable. He had crossed the superstitious line that no man could ever re-cross. He had violated the safe haven of El Aqua Dios. The pistolero had committed the final perversion, an act so vile he would be branded for the remainder of this life and the life to come. Well, that wasn't good enough for Shiloh. He had to find them and get the boy back. Alive.

CHAPTER X

Colonel Sam Mattox untangled himself from his bed companion's arms and bolted upright in bed, more than a little annoyed at the loud banging on his bedroom door. Dull light filtering through the window told him it was just breaking day.

"What is it?" he growled angrily, palming the pistol lying on a bedside table.

"Señor," the voice of one of the guards called through the closed door, "Come quickly."

Hurriedly pulling on his pants, he shrugged his arms through the attached suspenders and padded barefooted toward the door, still carrying the pistol.

"Sam," Romano Diego said sleepily, sitting up in bed. "What is it?"

"It's nothing," he assured her. "Go back to sleep."

Flinging the door open, the Colonel prepared himself to give the guard a severe tongue lashing until his gaze fell on the two items in the guard's hands. In one hand the short Mexican held a heavy rope fashioned into a hangman's noose. His other hand held out a shiny bayonet.

The Colonel's mouth dropped open. His eyes widened in

shock. He stood, staring speechless. Immediate recognition flushed through his mind and mirrored in his face. There could be no mistake, he knew. It was the one called Shiloh.

But how could that be? He himself had seen the Rebel hanged. He couldn't possibly be alive. Yet, the message was unmistakable.

"Where?" he bellowed at the top of his voice.

The small Mexican guard drew back in the face of the Colonel's fury. He stammered and stuttered, finally getting the words out.

"Stuck in the front gate, señor," the frightened guard managed. "When we opened the doors this morning, they were there."

"El Lobo," Mattox yelled like a madman. "Tell El Lobo I want to see him immediately."

"But he is not here, señor," the guard said. "He rode out yesterday with four of his men. They have gone to Chihuahua looking for more riders to hire."

The Colonel flew into a tirade. He slammed the door shut in the guard's face, stomped over to snatch his boots from the floor and pulled them on.

"What's happening?" the woman asked hysterically, climbing from the bed and pulling on a robe to cover her nakedness.

"Shut up!" he screamed at her. "Just shut your mouth. I've got to think."

He hurried from the room, pulling on his shirt. The two guards were huddled together near the front gate, they straightened as the Colonel approached.

"You—Hermano," Mattox ordered, "ride to the barracks. Bring Duncan, Folsom, Phillips, and Adams to me right away. Hurry. Tell them to bring every man that rides for us. Go!"

The guard ran to the corral, hurriedly saddled his horse, and galloped from the compound.

"Must I do everything myself around here?" the Colonel shouted, wheeling and stalking toward the house.

By the time he threw on his clothes and stormed back outside, his saddled horse was waiting. He twisted his head nervously from side to side, sweeping the compound with a searching gaze. The Rebel could be anywhere, he thought to himself, even here. He hurriedly climbed into the saddle and spurred the black gelding through the open front gate.

Two dozen riders galloped to meet him, pulling their mounts to a skidding stop near the river's edge.

"Duncan. Phillips." Mattox shouted. "Take half the men. Folsom, Adams, you and the rest come with me. It's the Rebel we hung back at Camp Douglas. He's still alive and he's here. Scour the countryside. He must not leave Mexico alive. This time we will make sure. Bring his head to me. I want to see it with my own eyes. Go!"

A thumbnail moon hung low in the western sky and filtered through a long caravan of clouds that drifted across its face shrouding the desert with near pitch blackness. Shiloh felt a sick awareness that knotted his stomach. His chances of tracking El Lobo and his men in the darkness were slim to none.

He hauled back on Buck's reins and leaped from the saddle. Pressing his ear to the sand, he listened intently—not a sound. Darkness and the desert were his enemies. The kidnappers had been swallowed up by the night.

Crestfallen, he mounted and turned his horse back toward the village. There was nothing else to do but wait until first light to set out after them. He dreaded to tell Consuela.

A crowd had gathered outside the small adobe hut that Consuela's aunt called home. Anxious faces lifted with hope as Shiloh rode up, but quickly gave way to looks of bitter disappointment as he dropped his eyes and sadly shook his head. He climbed wearily from the saddle.

Consuela could no longer choke back the tears. She rushed into his arms. Her small body heaved against him as great racking sobs shook her. She pillowed her head on his broad shoulder, her face turned into the warm, whiskered crook of his neck. His strong hands splayed across her back. Broad, rough hands holding her together while she cried. Strong, capable hands offering consolation. He seemed gentle and solid and safe.

"I'll find him," he whispered into her sweet smelling hair. "If it's the last thing I do, I'll find him and bring him back to you."

Truth she had smothered with her grief now slithered to the surface.

"He's taken Benito so I will come to him," she choked out with a shaky breath.

"It ain't gonna happen," he said, the very thought of it sending a chill racing up his spine.

"I'm afraid for my son," she said, and he could hear the tears in her voice. "El Lobo has said if he can't have me, none will. I'm frightened of what he might do to Benito if I do not do what he wants."

"What he will do, he will do," Shiloh told her, "Whether or not you went to him. Come first light I will track them down and do my best to rescue the boy. Is there somewhere I could rent a bed for the night?"

"There is a small sleeping room behind the cantina," she said, brushing away her tears with the back of her hand. "I will tell my father and show you where it is."

She hurried into her aunt's casa and was gone only a moment.

"Father said you are welcome to use the room for as long as you like. Come. I will show you."

They walked side by side. Shiloh led the buckskin as they made their way around the cantina to a tiny adobe lean-to.

"Father uses it to store supplies. He added a small cot for an occasional traveler that sometimes wander through."

"It will do just fine," he assured her.

He lifted a stirrup, loosened the cinch straps, and slid the saddle from the gelding's back.

"I want to get on the trail by first light," he told her.

He tied the long reins to a small hitching post and patted his horse on the neck. Consuela stood nearby, leaning her back against the small building. Her presence sent tingling chill bumps crawling over his skin. His gaze took her in. Her face shone with a rare deep beauty that not even her sorrow could disguise.

"I'm going with you," she said decisively.

"No," Shiloh said flatly. "I'll have a better chance of getting the boy back if I go alone. Stay here where it's safe."

She said nothing more on the subject but a sideways glance told him she hadn't given up on the idea.

"Consuela," he stammered out, suddenly tongue-tied but feeling an overwhelming need to put voice to the feelings that were screaming out inside him.

He toed the sand with a boot, his eyes staring at the mark in the sand as though he had just discovered this new ability. His mind struggled to find the right words before he continued. He cleared his throat and swallowed twice before he could squeeze words past the knot in his throat.

"When...when this is all over, there's a question in me that needs an answer."

The soft rustle of cloth and the crunch of tiny feet on sand caused him to lift his face. She stood before him, so close he could smell her freshness.

Starlight sparkled in her dark, inquisitive eyes as they searched for and found his. A serious look replaced the crooked little smile on her beautiful face as she stepped even closer.

He could feel the heat from her body radiating across the small distance that separated them, warming his own. His heartbeat jolted against his chest. His blood coursed hot through his veins. He caught his breath in quick gulps, his lungs suddenly devoid of air.

Consuela breached the slight space between them, lifted her arms and laced his neck. Her face tilted as she pulled him to her. Lips as soft as rose petals parted to welcome his. He tasted the sweet, heated mingling of their breath. He took possession of her mouth, claiming and savoring, demanding, yet tender. A low moan escaped her throat. The crush of her mouth grew urgent and wonderful with undreamed of promises.

His heart pounded. A warm flush surged through him like a hot chill. His quickened breathing came in sharp, staccato gasps. He returned her pressure and heard a soft sigh as their bodies molded as one. They clung together in the darkness in an embrace they both needed desperately.

They alone existed. Everything and everyone else were a part of the other world locked outside themselves. Their eternity lasted only a few fleeting moments, but Shiloh knew in his heart those moments had altered both their destinies.

Slipping free, she turned reluctantly, her fingers trailing along the tips of his and was gone. He listened to the soft, running crunch of her sandaled feet until the sound was lost in the night wind.

They had ridden hard for the better part of four hours. A glance upward told El Lobo it was near midnight. It was clear no one could have followed them in the darkness. For the last hour a plan had formulated in his mind. He reined to a stop.

Exhaustion had overcome the small boy in the saddle in front of him. His small body draped limply, held in place by the pistolero's left arm.

"Rodrigo," the bandit leader told one of his men, "take Domingo's horse, he can double up with Julio. The Americano will follow us at daybreak. I want you to circle back to the village. Wait until well after he leaves then go to Consuela. Tell her if she don't come with you I will kill the boy. She will come. Bring her to my cabin in the mountains. Make sure you are not followed. Go. Do not fail me, amigo."

"We will not fail," the one called Rodrigo assured him, taking up the reins of Domingo's vacated horse.

"Pancho," El Lobo said, swinging his attention to the fourth of his men.

"Take the boy to my mountain cabin and watch him. Do not let him out of your sight. I must ride to Chihuahua to meet the new pistoleros I have recruited. We will meet you at the cabin."

El Lobo listened to the sound of the retreating horses. A cruel smile curled one corner of his mouth. He was pleased with himself. He would have his woman and kill the Americano when he came for the boy. He jammed spurs to his mount and rode on into the night alone.

Shiloh jerked upright from the woven rope bottom cot and blinked his eyes clear. A hint of light from a pale gray sky slanted its way through the open doorway. Swinging stocking feet to the sand floor, he cleared his throat and shook his head to clear the cobwebs of both sleep and those reoccurring nightmares from his mind.

A pleasing grin crinkled the corners of his mouth as the recollection of last night's intimacy with Consuela flooded his being. He had never met another woman like her.

Somewhere a rooster crowed, setting off a chorus of answers announcing the breaking of a new day. Then the reality of the task that lay before him rushed over him. Somehow he must rescue the boy. That was gonna take some doing.

Shaking out his boots and stomping them on, he sleeved into his shirt and tucked it into his pants. He strapped his two guns in place and pulled the ragged serape over his head. Clamping his Confederate cavalry hat onto his head, he strode outside.

He poured the feedbag half full from the grain he had bought from the trading post. He slipped Buck's bridle off and strapped the feedbag over the buckskin's muzzle, then retied the sack behind his saddle.

The village was waking up by the time he was saddled and his gelding had finished eating. Shiloh led his horse to the well and filled the trough. He washed his own face and capped off his canteens.

He aimed a parting look toward the small casa where Consuela and her father lived, then booted a stirrup, and swung up into the saddle. Reining the gelding toward the west, he heeled his mount into a short lope.

The kidnapper's trail was plain to see in the soft sand. A blind man could have followed it. It was easy to follow, maybe too easy. Where would they take the boy? What would El Lobo do? Would he leave men behind to ambush him? Shiloh cast a weary eye at every swag, every sand dune, every clump of mesquite.

An hour passed. Then two. The tracks swung east in the direction of Chihuahua. Did the pistolero have a house there? He rode on.

Gray clouds hid the boiling sun. A hot wind picked up, driving stinging particles of dust across the sea of sand and causing horse and rider to bend their heads low. Only the whistling wind broke the silence that enveloped the land. The wind was his enemy. It wiped the desert clean, obliterating the tracks.

Confound the luck, he thought. *What now?* All he could do was keep heading the same direction the tracks had been going before they were erased by the wind.

It was nearing sundown when he rode into the sleepy town

of Chihuahua. He had been there before. He had stopped and spent the night in the little flea-bitten hotel during his wandering and searching for the Colonel. That's when he had picked up the information that led him west, before he had stumbled onto the village of El Aqua Dios. He'd ask around, hoping somebody knew El Lobo and where he might find him.

Experience had taught him there were usually two sources of information in any small town. One was the livery, the other was the saloon.

He headed for the first.

"Buenas Noches, señor," the weathered old Mexican liveryman mumbled as Shiloh reined up at the dilapidated adobe stable.

"Buenas Noches," Shiloh replied, stepping stiffly from the saddle. "Double grain, water, and rub him down good. I'll be over at the hotel."

Shiloh fished a dollar from his pocket, handed it to the old fellow, then produced another and held it up for the man to see.

"I'm looking for a fellow," he said hoarsely. "Goes by the name of El Lobo. Ever heard of him?"

A look of fear swept over the old Mexican's face. His head followed his dark eyes as they flicked from side to side. The man eyed the extra dollar in Shiloh's fingers longingly . . .then shook his head.

"No, señor. I know no one by that name."

Shiloh knew he was lying. He added another dollar to the second. "Think harder," he prompted.

The old timer's eyes caressed the coins in Shiloh's hand. He licked his lips and sleeved his mouth. His eyes swept a wide circle. The mask of fear on his face was pushed aside by greed. His wrinkled face tightened as he turned his head toward a horse stall near the back. Shiloh's gaze followed. In the stall stood a black and white pinto.

Shiloh slipped the two dollars into the old fellow's gnarled hand and lifted the thong from his saddle horn that held the Stevens sawed off double barrel. Threading an arm through the leather thong, he looped it over his shoulder, allowing the shotgun to hang down under his left arm, covering it from sight with the faded serape.

This El Lobo must be one bad hombre, Shiloh thought, as he headed toward the hotel. Twilight had settled. Shadows lengthened along the dusty street. Local townspeople made their way somewhere, but didn't seem to be in any hurry to get there. Life was slow, hard, and short in Mexico, he decided.

Music from a Mexican mariachi band blared through the open door of a two-story cantina as he neared. It drew his interest. He headed that way.

A dozen or more horses stood hipshot at the hitching rail in front of the cantina. Shiloh eyed them closely. Most were sleek, long legged stock, born and bred to run. These weren't the mounts of a working vaquero. A whole year's steady wages wouldn't buy one of those horses. Big-horned Mexican saddles trimmed with silver conchos adorned their backs. Saddle boots held the latest model Henry repeating rifles. Shiloh thumbed traveling thongs from both of his pistols and pushed through the open door.

His entrance drew the attention of every man in the room. Two dozen heads swung his way. Tough looking hombres with hard, searching eyes raked him with a critical gaze as he strode to an empty table near the front wall of the dimly lit room.

An attractive, dark-eyed señorita in a long red skirt and a low cut white blouse sauntered up to his table. She bent low over the table, offering a free view of her womanly attributes as she wiped the table with a dirty rag. Her flirting eyes pinned him with a lingering look as she flashed an inviting smile.

"Do you understand English?" he asked in a raspy voice.

"Si, señor," she replied. "Of course."

"Good. Do you have food that's fit to eat?"

"Si, señor," she said, trading the original faked smile with one that looked genuine. "We have the best food in all Chihuahua."

"Well, bring me a plateful of whatever you got and coffee to wash it down."

She spun on her toes and headed toward a double door opening in the back wall. She walked with an easy stride, her red skirt swishing from side to side with every exaggerated movement. Shiloh's presence was temporarily forgotten as most every eye in the place followed her all the way to the kitchen opening.

While he waited on his food, he allowed his gaze to crawl over the men in the room. These were hard men. Men who wore pistols in low slung, tied down holsters and most likely knew how to use them. Many wore leather bandoleers criss-crossing their chests. These were men whose nervous alertness questioned everyone and trusted no one, especially a gringo this deep into Mexico.

As in most every group, one stood out from the rest. These men were no exception. He was young, no older than his late teens. Most would call him handsome. An easy, devilish smile revealed pearly-white, perfect teeth. Dark, flashing eyes showed through tight eyelids. The flawless skin of his face was crowned by coal-black, wavy hair. A black hat with silver conchos hung down his back by a leather neck cord.

He lounged against the bar with two others, all sipping tequila. He wore a pearl handled Colt tied low on his left hip. He laughed easily at something one of them said, but his gaze was fixed directly on Shiloh. He had an overpowering, reckless energy about him. There stood trouble waiting to happen, Shiloh allowed.

The band struck up a lively tune and the pretty señorita in the red skirt strolled to the center of the floor and paused. Her head looked down. One arm rose over her head, posing for a long moment. Suddenly she began twirling on the ball of one bare foot. Her full skirt billowed out, revealing bare, shapely legs.

She broke into a dance. Every movement blended perfectly with the beat of the music. She moved about the room, gliding near the watchers, smiling seductively, trailing a hand along their face, tempting, teasing, tantalizing. She was fully aware of her beauty and she used it to its fullest.

The music built. Her movements quickened. She spun. She dipped. Two five string guitars beat a driving rhythm. An accordion added the melody. A trumpet blared. The band's volume swelled to a final crescendo, as the dancer began a prolonged twirling finish. Around and around she spun, ending up near the handsome young pistolero at the bar.

As the music stopped, he took a step forward, swept an arm around the girl's waist, and pulled her roughly to him. One hand caught up a handful of her long black hair and jerked her mouth to his. Her arms circled his neck. His compadres cheered.

She loosed herself from the young man, laughed, and trailed tantalizing fingers along his dark cheek as she made her way to the kitchen. In a moment she returned with a plate of steaming-hot Mexican food. She sat the plate before Shiloh and poured his cup full from a blackened coffeepot.

"Did you enjoy my dance, señor?" she purred, standing uncomfortably close to his chair.

"It was exciting," he said, lifting his gaze to look into her face.

"Exciting?" she questioned, smiling. "Did it excite you, señor?"

"I reckon it would excite most any man that wasn't dead yet. Maybe even a few of them."

"Would you like to buy me a drink?" she asked pointedly. "Or we could go upstairs."

"Some other time, maybe," he said, shrugging away her suggestion. "But I would like to ask you a question."

"Si," she said, searching his eyes with her own. "What would you like to know?"

"Ever hear of a fellow they call El Lobo?"

The girl suddenly straightened. A frown creased her forehead and the smile vanished.

"I must go," she said curtly, wheeling and heading toward the back.

The young Mexican at the bar had been watching and stepped to intercept the girl. They talked for a moment. The girl turned and walked away, twisting a quick look of concern over her shoulder at Shiloh. The handsome young pistolero strode over and stopped a few feet short of Shiloh's table.

"You are Americano?" the man asked, a friendly looking smile appearing on his face.

"I reckon so," Shiloh replied in a loud whisper. "Is that a problem?"

"Oh, no, señor," the fellow said. "Rosetta says you were asking about a man named El Lobo. What is your business with him?"

"Do you know him?" Shiloh asked, ignoring the man's own question.

"Si, I know him," the man said, using a tone that said he wasn't especially proud of the fact. "Most of the men in this room are men he has just hired."

"Are you one of his men?" Shiloh asked.

"I am no one's man, señor," the young fellow said. "I am my own man. Are you here to go to work for the Colonel?"

"Not hardly," Shiloh said, taking a sip of coffee and peering over the rim of the cup at the young Mexican. "I'm here to kill him."

"You are either a very brave man or you have been eating loco weed," the Mexican said. "Could I buy you a drink?"

"Don't drink nothing stronger than coffee," Shiloh said, pointing to a chair with his fork, "but you're welcome to sit a spell."

"I am Rico Lopez," the young fellow said, scraping out a chair and folding into it.

"Some call me Shiloh."

"Why do you seek El Lobo?" the young man asked again.

"He kidnapped a little boy yesterday," Shiloh said. "I want him back. Do you know where I can find him?"

"Si, señor," Rico told him, glancing past him. "If you sit where you are sitting, he will find you. He is upstairs with Selene, has been for awhile."

"Well, what do you know about that?" Shiloh said. "Why do I get the feeling you don't particularly like the Colonel or his man, El Lobo."

"Don Diego was my uncle. He was one of the greatest men I ever knew. He owned a great hacienda on the San Miguel River where it runs through the Sierra Madre Mountains. When the Colonel and his men came to Mexico, they killed my uncle and all those loyal to him. The Colonel took over his hacienda as his own. The gringo pig now sleeps with my uncle's wife. I myself would kill him if I had the chance."

Shiloh forked a jaw full of the steaming tortillas from his plate and chewed on it as well as what the young Mexican had said.

"You got any idea where El Lobo might have taken the boy?" Shiloh asked around a mouthful of tortillas.

"I heard some talk about him having a cabin somewhere upstream from my uncle's hacienda. Someplace back in the mountains I think, but I don't know exactly where. Are you going there?" Rico asked.

"Yep," Shiloh said, taking a long sip of coffee. "Just as soon as I'm finished here."

"You going to take on the whole bunch?" the young fellow asked, concern creasing his forehead.

"If I have to," Shiloh said. "Is Rosetta your girl?"

"She is anyone's girl if they have the price," he said, showing teeth with a wide smile.

"She's very beautiful," Shiloh said, flicking a quick gaze toward the steps leading upstairs.

"I have decided, señor." Rico suddenly said, pushing back his chair. "I am going to help you. Me and my two friends will see that no one else takes a part when El Lobo comes down."

"I ain't asking you to get yourself killed on my account," Shiloh said, eyeing the young Mexican.

"I was born looking for a place to die," Rico said, flashing one of those devil-may-care smiles of his.

"I'd be much obliged," Shiloh said, reaching a hand to the young Mexican.

The handshake was firm and friendly. Rico Lopez turned and sauntered back to the bar. He whispered something low to his two friends. They nodded understanding, turned around with their back to the bar, and shifted their drinks to their left hands.

Shiloh had just scraped the last mouthful of food from his plate and poured himself another cup of steaming coffee when he saw Rico's eyes cut to the stairway. He, too, looked that way. He took a sip of coffee then stood.

El Lobo came strutting down the stairs. His large Mexican spurs rattled as he descended slowly. As he did, he buttoned the top button of his shirt, adjusted his hat, and stopped to knot the leg tie-downs to the pistols that rode low on both hips. When he looked up from that task, he spotted Shiloh.

For a long moment El Lobo stood motionless, three steps from the bottom. His haunting, wolf's eyes swept a circle of the room. Seeming pleased with what he saw, a smirk widened, lifting one corner of his slanted mouth and his eyes locked directly on Shiloh. He took the remaining three steps slowly, his gaze never straying.

One of his newly hired pistoleros stepped to meet him. El Lobo's long arm brushed the man aside. Spurs jingled with each lingering step as he stalked toward Shiloh, stopping twenty feet shy.

"So, gringo," he snarled wickedly, like a shewolf contending for a bone. "We meet again."

"You knew we would," Shiloh whispered. "Where's the boy?"

"He's alive...for now," the man said, a self-satisfying smile curling a lip. "I'm going to kill you, gringo."

Shiloh stood easy, feet planted, knees slightly bent, his right hand hung loosely near the Colt on his right hip. His left thumb casually hooked the belt at his waist, his unseen fingers resting on the matching Colt in the belly holster, hidden from view by the tattered edge of the worn serape.

"That's big talk from such a little man." Shiloh whispered hoarsely, deliberately goading, hoping to stoke the fire of the man's wrath, knowing anger can disrupt a man's timing as well as his thinking. "I got the idea you only picked on helpless women and little boys."

The smirking smile dropped from El Lobo's face. The smile just fell, like a rock down a well. Shiloh's unwavering gaze locked on the man's evil eyes, eyes he imagined would belong only to the devil himself, eyes of a man for whom death held no fear and possibly some pleasure, eyes that he knew would tell him when the man was about to draw. For an eternity, which measured only in seconds, they stood facing each other.

Quiet filled the room. Death hovered like a heavy fog, waiting to see who it would claim this night. Shiloh wasn't afraid of death. It had been his constant companion since he was nineteen. It had ridden at his side all during the war. It had snatched comrades from within an arm's length during numerous battles. Many were the nights it had crept silently into his barracks at the prison camp and stolen friends away. No, he had skirted the ragged edges of death too often, he had been haunted by its messengers too many sleepless nights in too many nightmares to be frightened by its nearness now.

Suddenly he saw it—the slight squinting of El Lobo's eyes, the tightening of his lips; he was about to draw.

In a blur of swiftness, the pistolero's right hand swept upward, palming the Colt without pause. A thumb eared back its hammer even as its dark nose arched upward. Shiloh's right hand didn't move. His left hand did.

The pearl handled Colt appeared as if by magic from under the worn and faded serape. It barked twice in rapid succession.

The twin blasts rocked the room. Two dark, sightless eyes appeared in El Lobo's chest, then transformed into fountains, squirting red blood with each beat of his heart. He staggered from the force of the double impact. His spurs jingled as his booted feet tried in vain to break his backwards fall, a dancer's step to an unheard melody. A look of shock and surprise swept the Mexican's ugly face, like he couldn't believe what had just happened. His unfired pistol curled from his fingers and clattered to the floor. A reaching hand clutched his chest and pulled away. The man's gaze dropped to stare unbelieving at the blood that clung there, then rolled upward.

He died on the way to the floor, his shadowy soul hurrying to take its place in the line of marching dead that would return to visit Shiloh for all the nights to come.

Shiloh's second pistol was in his right hand. The noses of his twin Colts followed his darting eyes around the room. His gaze revealed a dozen pistoleros, their hands frozen motionless, halfway to their weapons.

Rico Lopez and his two friends stood near the bar, their pistols out and covering the surprised Mexicans.

"These hombres will not trouble you, amigo," the handsome young man said, smiling. "My compadres and I will see they do not follow you."

"I'd be much obliged," Shiloh told his newfound friend, leathering his pistols and turning toward the door. "Maybe we'll meet again down the trail."

"Adios, Amigo," Rico said, his gaze never leaving the Mexican pistoleros.

"Adios," Shiloh called back over his shoulder as he pushed hurriedly out the door.

CHAPTER XI

Consuela woke with a start. The early morning sun beaming through the window of her father's small casa told her she had overslept. Shiloh would already be gone. She had intended to be up before he left. She had wanted to bid him goodbye.

The night was far spent before sleep had come. Conflicting emotions had caused her to toss and turn. Tears of concern for Benito had torn at her, racking her body with great, uncontrollable sobs. Feelings of guilt and helplessness haunted her. What should she do? What could she do?

She knew full well why El Lobo had taken Benito. He didn't want him, he wanted her. If she must, she would gladly sacrifice her life for her son. Perhaps if she went to him, agreed to be his woman, Benito would not be harmed.

But what of Shiloh? She had allowed him to set out on an impossible quest. Could he possibly succeed? Could he find Benito? Even if he did would her son still be alive? Could Shiloh somehow rescue him without losing his own life? All these emotions and more clouded her mind. Fresh tears breached the rims of her lashes. A sob squirmed its way up her throat.

Shaking her head, she climbed quickly from her small cot and stepped to the window. The back of a curved finger pushed aside the plain white curtains and she peered out.

The early morning sun baked hot into the white sand. A few white clouds drifted lazily across the blue sky. Somewhere a child's happy laughter filled the air. A goat bleated, a rooster crowed, and Señora Perez and her new husband were arguing again. Just another typical morning in El Aqua Dios.

But this wasn't just another day. Nothing would ever be like it was before. Her son had been taken from her and—

She drew a shaky breath as the events of the night before flooded her mind. Her eyes clamped shut. A hand lifted to her mouth. Fingers traced slowly along her sensitive lips. *The kiss...was it only in my mind? Was it just another of my frequent fantasies? It must have been just a dream. I must have imagined it all..*

No! She scolded herself. *I could never have just imagined something so wonderful. It did happen. The things I felt were real. His kiss awakened yearnings I never thought I would have again.* The reality of it brought a smile to her lips as her eyes fluttered open.

"Shiloh," the name worked its way up her throat and fell from her lips aloud, suddenly feeling an overwhelming need to speak the name, to feel the shape of it in her mouth, to hear the sound of it on her voice.

Did she dare hope this big, handsome Americano might feel about her like she confessed to herself she felt about him?

Through the window she saw her father on his way to the cantina. She must hurry. There was much to do. Lifting a wooden bucket, she poured water into a tin wash basin and quickly bathed, dressed, and hurried from the small adobe dwelling they called home.

Lost in her reveling, she noticed, but failed to pay attention to, the rider sliding his horse down the sandy hillside behind the mission. When he kicked his mount into a trot and headed directly toward her she jerked a look. Recognition came quickly, and with it a hot surge of fear swept through her. The burly, bearded pistolero was one of El Lobo's men. A scream burst from her throat. She broke into a run. He quickly overtook her. Leaning far over in his saddle the big Mexican snaked a strong arm around her waist and swept her across the saddle in front of him.

Twisting a look backward as they galloped away, she saw her father run from the cantina, stumble forward a few steps, and drop to his knees in the sand. Her heart broke as she saw his head lift skyward, his helpless arms stretched after them, his pleading screams faded swiftly into the distance.

The rumble of thirty galloping horses disturbed the quietness of the desert. Dust from churning hooves rose in a great cloud and was slow to settle. The blistering mid morning sun cooked into the powdery white sand and bounced shimmering heat waves upward, distorting the outline of the little village ahead.

Colonel Sam Mattox sat straight and tall in the saddle, his gaze fixed on the tiny village in the distance. His sweat-soaked black gelding's nostrils flared and a guttural sound emitted from deep in the big horse's throat with each stride. Lesser horses in the ragged line behind him began to falter and slow. They had held the murderous pace all morning.

As they drew near the village of El Aqua Dios a wave of the Colonel's arm sent Frank Duncan circling to the right with ten men. Ten more riders peeled from the column and swung left led by Bill Jeffcoat. George Folsom and the remaining half-dozen pistoleros followed the Colonel straight into the village.

A small herd of goats milling on the outskirts scattered from the path of the charging horses. Chickens cackled and scurried from under the horse's hooves in a flurry of batting wings. Village people stepped outside at the sound, took one look, then quickly gathered children inside and closed wooden doors. Armed riders poured between buildings from every direction. The village was surrounded.

Sam Mattox reined up in front of the small mission as Father Sebastian, led by a young bareheaded boy, stepped through the door.

"I'm Colonel Sam Mattox," he announced, his voice ringing with authority.

"I know who you are," the blind old padre said. "Why have you come here with all these men?"

"I'm looking for an Americano who calls himself, Shiloh. I believe he is here."

"No, there is no Americano here except those who came with you. But even if there were, this is a sanctuary of God. Those who defile it will feel the wrath of God." His voice swelled to a near shout as he said the words.

Hearing a murmuring from his men, the Colonel swiveled in his saddle. His slow, threatening glare crawled over each of them. He was well aware of their silly superstitions about the tiny village. They sat their saddles, their rifles propped on a leg and pointed upward. He saw their nervousness. He watched their eyes cut from side to side, a visible uneasiness plain on every face. It was as if they were trying to decide which would be worse, the wrath of God, of the wrath of the Colonel.

"Where is he, padre?" Mattox demanded harshly.

"I do not know," the padre replied.

"I don't have time to play games, holy man," the Colonel shouted, his face flushing red with anger.

"God does not play games," Father Sebastian said evenly.

"Either someone is hiding him or you know where he has gone, either way, you will tell me what I want to know."

"It is true he was here," Father Sebastian said. "One of your own men took one of our young boys. The Americano you seek rode out to find him. That is all we know."

"Round up everybody," Mattox shouted, waving his arms in every direction. "Men, women, children, everybody! Bring them all here. Someone knows where he is."

It took only minutes for the pistoleros to gather the villagers that had not already fled into the desert. They huddled nervously together in front of the mission. Mothers clutched frightened children in protective arms. Stooped old men supported their aged wives. Hatless peons stood helplessly, their eyes turned to the ground. Father Sebastian stepped from the group and shuffled to stand before them.

"I have told you everything we know," he said meekly.

"You're lying!" the Colonel's rage sounded in his raised voice. "You're all lying! You will tell me where he is or I will hang every last one of you!"

"These people have done nothing," the padre pleaded. "They know nothing of the Americano. Do not harm them."

"Hang them!" Mattox screamed.

Shiloh saw the dark specks circling high and slow in a cloudless sky over the distant shimmering village of El Aqua Dios. They appeared as mere smudges against the blinding glare of a noon sun. Their presence could only mean one thing. His stomach knotted.

Giving the lead rope to El Lobo's black and white pinto another wrap around his saddle's apple, Shiloh dug heels deep into the buckskin's flanks, lifting him into a hard gallop. His heart crawled into his throat as his gaze glued to the circling vultures, each lazy loop dropping them lower and lower.

Powdery plumes of dust puffed from pounding hooves as he galloped into the village. What he saw caused him to rein up hard. His stomach churned and a bitter bile rose into his throat. The shock of the sight took his breath away.

Two dozen lifeless bodies hung from the bell tower of the mission. Men, women, children, elderly, their corpses suspended by hastily fashioned nooses, rested against the adobe wall. Necks twisted grotesquely. Unseeing eyes stared. Bare feet dangled in the air. A scream strained for voice in his throat but was choked off by the sheer inhumanity of the sight.

Great billows of anger surged over him as his gaze examined each body. He recognized the shopkeeper. There was the young goat herder, no more than ten or twelve years old. Señor Cordona, Consuela's father, hung next to his sister. Frantically, Shiloh's eyes searched. Where was Consuela?

A low groan from a corner of the building reached his hearing. His gaze swung there. The blind old padre lay in a crumpled heap. Grabbing a canteen, Shiloh leaped from his saddle and rushed to the holy man's side. Blood covered half his face where a pistol barrel had struck him.

Gently lifting the priest's head, Shiloh tipped the canteen to allow water to trickle onto the padre's dry lips.

"It's Shiloh," he whispered. "Can you hear me?"

The priest weakly nodded his head and licked to moisten his lips. His sightless eyes gave birth to silver tears and seemed to search Shiloh's face for an answer to the eternal question. . .why?

"Who did this?" Shiloh whispered through clenched teeth.

"The...Colonel," came the halting reply.

"Consuela?" Shiloh questioned. "What about Consuela?"

"The one called El Lobo," the padre forced through swollen lips. "His man took her yesterday."

It took awhile for Shiloh to care for the padre as best he could and see to his comfort. It took awhile longer for him and the few surviving villagers to complete the gruesome task of burying the dead in the little cemetery on the hill behind the mission. The day was far spent as he hung refilled canteens over his saddle horn and climbed wearily into the saddle.

Seeing and hearing what Colonel Mattox had done to the innocent villagers confirmed everything Shiloh knew of the man: that he was heartless, soulless, and sadistic.

He reined his buckskin around to face the setting sun. For a long moment he sat his saddle and stared absently at the crimson spikes as they faded behind the horizon. An overwhelming sadness washed over him. He watched as it slid quickly behind the sandy hill to the west of town as if embarrassed at man's inhumanity to man, anxious to put an end to the terrible day. Then, taking up the lead rope to the pinto, Shiloh determinedly set his face westward.

He rode all night, stopping only long enough to allow his horses to rest. First light found him watering in the San Miguel River in the rugged foothills of the Sierra Madre Mountains. By his reckoning, he was a good ten or twelve miles upstream of the Colonel's hacienda. His plan was to work along the mountain side of the river until he struck a trail leading into the mountains. He figured that was the only hope he had of finding El Lobo's mountain cabin that Rico Lopez had told him about. But first he had to get some rest. It had been two whole days since he had closed his eyes.

Reining his horses up the sloping riverbank, he threaded through a thick stand of young pine saplings and into a boulder strewn clearing. Weaving between house-size rocks, he found a grass covered opening that was completely surrounded with large, rocky outcroppings.

Satisfied with the place, he stepped down, and pulled the saddles from both horses so they could graze. Then he spread his bedroll and lay down for some much needed rest. He was bone weary.

They came, as they always did, in the familiar dregs of his dreams, the walking dead. They emerged from a thick fog, marching single file in an tightening circle around him. They stared. Their pleading, restless eyes fixed and unblinking, never wavering from this sleeping one. The one that had condemned them to an eternity without rest, an eternity suspended somewhere between heaven and hell.

Consuela stood in front of the rock fireplace stirring a pot of deer chili that hung from the lug pole. Silent tears scorched trails down her face, seeping hot and salty into her mouth. Since her arrival at El Lobo's cabin three days earlier, she had been given the task of preparing food for the five pistoleros, as well as for herself and her son.

Benito sat at a wooden table nearby. Consuela stirred the chili absently and watched as he and the slow thinking one called, Pancho, stacked tiny wooden, sticks the pistolero had cut for him to play with. The two laughed happily as the little stick house they were building fell flat. She was struck by how contented her son seemed. He is safe, she thought, at least for now, and we are together, that is the most important thing. She was glad the young boy wasn't aware of the danger they were in, or the uncertain future they both faced.

A rush of emotions swept through her. She felt helpless. They were many miles from El Aqua Dios. No one knew where they were, even she didn't know, it had been pitch dark when they arrived. She only knew they were somewhere in the mountains and that there was little chance they could escape. Her and her son could die and none of her loved ones would even know of their death. She also knew what awaited her when El Lobo returned and her stomach rebelled at the thought.

She thought of Shiloh and a warm feeling flushed over her. Wonder where he is? Wonder what he is doing right now? How long will he search for us before giving up?

She had never felt for anyone, not even her late husband, the way she felt about this Americano. She loved him, she knew that without a doubt. She had dared hope they had a future together. He had asked her to go with him to his country, but that was all gone now.

Dropping her head, she wept silently, muffling her sobs with her hand. Her body shook with spasms of hopelessness. Grief twisted her insides, wringing from her any hopes of a better future for her son, indeed, any hope for her own happiness.

Tearing futile thoughts from her mind, she swung her attention to the pistolero at the table. He was young, no older than herself. He seemed to be a child trapped in a man's body. He had a pleasant smile and an easy way about him. He had been good to her and Benito since they came, looking out for them, seeing to their needs.

"How did you get involved with El Lobo?" she asked the young pistolero. "You're not like the others."

The young man raised his eyes to look at her for a long moment before answering.

"Why do you say that?" he asked. "I am like the others. I am a pistolero."

"It's just... you've been so good to us. You seem to like my son and enjoy playing with him, and you— you don't look at me like the others do."

"You are El Lobo's woman. He would kill any man that would dare lay a hand on you."

"When will he be back?"

"Who knows?" he said, shrugging his shoulders. "He is like the wolf from which he is named. He comes, he goes. He is a very bad man, señorita. You must do what he says or he will kill both you and the boy."

"Could you—"

"I cannot help you, señorita," the young man said abruptly, cutting off her unasked question.

The door opened and the other four pistoleros stalked in.

They found a place on one of the wooden benches on either side of the table and sat down.

One of them, the one that had taken her from the village, swept the toy sticks from the table with a backhanded swipe of his hand before uncorking a bottle of mescal and taking a long swallow.

"I killed us another buck deer," the one called Domingo bragged. "We'll skin it after supper."

"Enough stirring," the big one called Rodrigo growled at her. "Give me a plate of that."

Benito jumped from the bench and ran to her in fear. She knelt and pulled her son to her and hugged him close.

"Go into the other room and wait there for me," she whispered into his ear. "I will bring you something to eat."

"Quit fussing over the boy and do what I told you," the big Mexican shouted.

As Benito left the room, she spooned a tin plate brimming full and slammed it on the table in front of the man, slouching the steaming-hot chili out onto his lap. He let out a scream and a string of curses as he drew back his hand to strike her.

"Rodrigo," Pancho intervened quickly. "El Lobo will kill you if you hit her."

For a long moment there was silence. The man hesitated, his big arm drawn back. Consuela stood her ground, prepared for the blow she expected would come but refusing to cower to this evil man. Finally, he lowered his hand and wiped the hot liquid from his lap with a sleeve.

It was then they heard the dog bark.

CHAPTER XII

A rifle shot awoke Shiloh from a restless sleep. His eyes snapped open and he blinked the world around him into focus. Bolting upright with the Stevens sawed-off shotgun in his hand, he listened intently. It came again. It was upstream and farther back in the mountains, he guessed a good two or three miles away at least.

Glancing up at the sun, he was shocked to see it dipping near the distant horizon. He had slept the day away. Quickly cinching up the saddles on both horses, he mounted and headed in the direction of the shots.

The towering mountains loomed over him. Crimson sprays from the setting sun shot skyward above the lofty peaks and painted a cloudless sky with golden rays of light. Twilight claimed the wooded valley as Shiloh picked his way cautiously through the trees.

A velvety curtain of darkness crept swiftly down the mountainside and shrouded the foothills. A quarter moon was already high and proud, restless from a long days rest. Stars peeked through the growing darkness as he broke out of a heavy stand of pine trees. He cast nervous looks over his shoulder as he rode, alert for any sound, any movement.

The smell of wood smoke reached his nostrils and he reined up. Quickly dismounting and palming the sawed-off double barrel, he tied his two horses at the edge of the thicket.

He found the log cabin in a small clearing surrounded by a heavy growth of large pine. Bellying down, he crawled slowly forward, finally snaking under a thick huckleberry bush. The cabin was solidly built and made of peeled logs. It looked to contain maybe three rooms. Smoke feathered upward from a rock chimney and bent sharply, swept away by a westerly wind. Light from two front windows cast square patches across the front porch and onto the ground.

A saddled bay stood hipshot, its reins wrapped around the top rail of a nearby corral. Inside the corral, a half-dozen horses milled about. *This has to be El Lobo's cabin*, he thought. *But is Consuela and Benito inside?*

Were they still alive? He could feel a squirm of concern and fear twisting in his gut.

A shadow moved in one of the light patches. A silhouette of a huge animal that looked more like a wolf than a dog raised its head and sniffed the air, then climbed to its feet and trotted from the porch. A low growl rumbled deep in its throat. Its eyes followed scent and fixed directly on the low clump of bushes where Shiloh lay. Well, so much for the element of surprise, he thought, as the big dog barked twice, then broke into a dead run toward him.

Not willing to risk a shot, Shiloh clawed the bayonet from his belt scabbard even as the animal leaped. It hurtled through the air. The impact of its weight bowled Shiloh over backwards. The snarling dog's bared fangs lunged for Shiloh's throat. At the last instant, he threw up his left forearm. Strong jaws clamped shut like a bear trap, sinking deep.

The savage beast shook its head fiercely, ripping flesh, tearing Shiloh's arm.

His bayonet flashed, plunging deep into the big dog's side and chest again and again, finally impaling the animal on the long blade. White froth dripped from the fatally wounded beast's snarling mouth onto Shiloh's face as the dog still struggled frantically to get at Shiloh's throat. Blood covered both man and beast from the gaping wounds in the animal and from Shiloh's torn arm. Finally, emitting a pitiful moan, the dog collapsed on top of Shiloh.

Shoving the dead carcass from him, Shiloh rolled to his knees in time to see two Mexican pistoleros burst from the now darkened cabin, with pistols drawn. He spun to his right, rolled once, and bellied flat as two bouquets of red blossomed from the darkness. He heard lead plow furrows in the ground he had just vacated. His own Colt was in his right hand and bucked twice, sending return fire at the fading red flashes of light. One shot went wide, slamming into the logs of the cabin with a thud. The other produced a soft smack, the familiar sound of a bullet striking flesh. A pistolero threw up his hands and staggered backwards.

The remaining shooter wheeled and headed for the front door, firing wildly as he ran. He didn't make it. The pistol in Shiloh's hand sounded twice more. The fleeing Mexican arched high on his tiptoes. He dropped his weapon and clawed at two new holes in his back, staggered forward another step, then sprawled face down in the dirt.

By the time the pistolero hit the ground Shiloh had holstered his pistol and ran to kneel beside the dying man. Grabbing a handful of long hair with his bleeding left hand and the man's cartridge belt with the other, he hoisted the Mexican up and shoved him through the open front door.

The explosion sounded like a cannon going off in the small cabin. The shotgun blast at close range cut the wounded man near in half and blew what was left of him back through the door.

The booming sound still echoed through the tall pines as Shiloh rounded the cabin at a run and kicked in the back door. Dim moonlight filtered through the open doorway and framed a crouching man behind an overturned table. He was busy reloading a shotgun.

"Drop it or die!" Shiloh gritted out hoarsely.

The man made the last mistake he would ever make. He twisted his body to bring the shotgun around. Shiloh's own shotgun boomed once. The force of the heavy buckshot lifted the pistolero up and over the table, depositing his mangled body several feet away.

Galloping hooves sounded from the corral. Shiloh raced to the back door in time to see the back end of a fleeing horse and rider being swallowed up by the darkness. There went number four, he thought, wheeling back into the cabin. He'll have every pistolero in Mexico looking for us. By Shiloh's reckoning, there was another one somewhere, maybe two.

The acrid stench of gun smoke filled the room and burned his throat with each struggled breath. He sleeved watering eyes and squinted through the darkness, straining his hearing for any sound, any movement.

Awareness of the hurt in his left arm drew his attention to it. His shirtsleeve was blood-soaked. Jerking the bandanna from around his neck he looped it above his elbow. Without wavering his searching gaze, he used his teeth to draw it tight and tied it off to stem the bleeding.

Noticing the door to the third room closed, he flattened his back against the log wall and inched to one side of the door.

"Consuela," he called out in a loud whispered voice. "It's Shiloh. Are you in there?"

"Si," came the frightened reply. "We are here."

"Is anyone with you?"

"Si, Pancho is here. He is a friend. Do not harm him, por favor?"

"Tell him to open the door and throw out his weapons."

A long minute passed. Finally the door opened slowly. A pistol slid through the door opening.

"Consuela...tell him to come through the door backwards with both hands on top of his head."

Shiloh could hear her giving instructions in their own language. In a moment, a small framed Mexican backed through the door with his hands on top of his hatless head. Shiloh stuck the nose of the double barrel in the fellow's back and checked for hideout weapons with his free hand. He found none.

Consuela stepped quickly through the door leading Benito by the hand. She wrapped both arms around Shiloh's waist and hugged him close.

Shiloh ruffled the boy's hair and hugged him close with one arm. Alive. They were both alive and safe, at least for now.

"Reckon you could find a lamp or candle or something?" he asked her.

"Si," she said, hurrying toward a small table near a front window.

In a minute the room was bathed in yellowish light from a coal oil lamp. Shiloh allowed his eyes a moment to drink in the image of her standing there. His heart leaped inside his chest at the sight.

The Mexican still stood nearby with his back to Shiloh and his hands on top of his head. He looked young, too young to be one of El Lobo's pistoleros.

"You called him a friend," Shiloh said. "Is he one of El Lobo's men?"

"Si," Consuela said, "but he tried to help us. He is not like the others."

Shiloh saw the young fellow cut a long look at what was left of his two compadres, then quickly turn his head away. He couldn't say he blamed the boy. It wasn't a pretty sight.

"You are hurt," she said, noticing Shiloh's bloody arm and stepping quickly to examine his injury.

"It's nothing," he assured her. "We've got to get moving.

One of them got away. Before long this place will be swarming with the Colonel's men."

"What about him?" she asked, nodding toward the young man.

Shiloh didn't answer for a few heartbeats. He fixed a look at the young Mexican as his mind explored all the options.

"Tell him I'll let him ride out if he'll just keep on riding. Tell him if I ever see him again I'll kill him."

In a rapid-fire rattle of Spanish she told him what Shiloh had said. The young fellow near broke his neck nodding agreement and saying the words over and over.

"Si, gracias. Muchas gracias! Muchas gracias, señor."

Striding to the lamp, Shiloh hurled it against the back wall of the room. The glass lamp shattered, splattering the coil oil over the dry logs. Flames leaped upward, licking its way toward the wooden ceiling beams.

A wave of Shiloh's arm sent the young fellow out the back door towards the corral in a run. Shiloh scooped the dead pistolero's long barreled shotgun from the floor as well as the leather ammunition belt full of double-ought shells. He looped the belt over a shoulder and settled the long gun in the crook of an arm. His other arm swept Benito up.

"Let's go!" he said over a shoulder as he headed for the front door.

They hurried to the little clearing where he had left his two horses. He lifted the boy and set him in the saddle of the pinto and turned to give Consuela a hand up. For the briefest of time their eyes met. Her deep chocolate eyes sparkled in the pale wash of moonlight. Their gazes met, and held, their hearts in their eyes. A shiver raced up his spine and his belly did a curious flip-flop.

"Muchas gracias," she whispered, a small smile lifting her pretty lips as she tiptoed to touch her soft lips to his.

More than anything he had ever wanted in the whole world he wanted to drop the shotgun and tell her the tragic news about her father and aunt and the other villagers, to encircle her with his arms and console her, to draw her to his chest, to feel her softness against him...to hold her. But this was not the time and this was not the place. Instead, his face tightened. He drew a shaky breath and looked away, then lifted her into the saddle.

He mounted and buried his heels in the big buckskin's flanks as he waved his arm in an urgent invitation.

"Stay close and ride hard," he shouted as loudly as he could. "We haven't got much time."

Twisting a look over his shoulder brought a pleasing feeling. The cabin was engulfed in a blazing inferno. That ought to buy us a few minutes, he thought as they hurried their horses down the narrow trail toward the river. They reined up occasionally to listen and make sure the way was clear before moving on. The trees along the foothills were tall and thick and would offer concealment if they encountered anyone.

As they neared the river, Shiloh reined up yet again to listen. The quiet of the forest was deafening. Night birds called above the steady drone of a myriad of locusts, producing a cacophony of sound. The buckskin stomped a hoof. The pinto snorted. They rode on.

Entering the belly-deep river, they reined up. The logical thing to do would be to head upstream and put as much distance as possible between them and the Colonel's hacienda, the direction the pistoleros would undoubtedly come from. Shiloh did the illogical. He headed downstream.

For a mile or more they splashed along in the river. Finally, he found what he was looking for and reined the buckskin out of the water onto a rocky ledge. Consuela urged the pinto to follow.

As they rode, Shiloh weighed his options, none of which seemed very promising. If they struck out across the desert, come daylight, the Colonel's men would surely discover their tracks and ride them down. If they went deeper into the mountains, it would only be a matter of time until they were tracked down. Facing odds of thirty or forty to one, their future didn't look too bright. The way he figured it, they had to make a stand, but where?

Then it hit him. The mountain. If they could only make it up the mountain without being seen, maybe they could wait them out for a few days until things cooled off a bit. If worse came to worse and they were discovered, at least he'd have a fighting chance to take a few of them with him. It was their best bet, and even that was kind of like drawing to an inside straight.

They rode along the riverbank nearest the mountains. The low brush and scrub willow thickets were thick and offered some measure of concealment. Then he heard them.

He hauled back on his reins and turned his horse sharply to the right, sending them into a grove of sycamore saplings and swung from the saddle. Consuela was beside him. Shiloh gentled the pinto and swiped his hat from his head, turning it upside down, he covered the pinto's nose to prevent him from nickering.

The low rumble of galloping horses sounded like distant thunder as it bounced off the mountain and reverberated along the river valley. A whole passel of pistoleros rode bunched up and coming hard as if the devil himself was on their trail. Perhaps he was. The Colonel led them on a black horse.

Shiloh bent low and peered through the thick bushes as the riders passed and disappeared from view.

"Let's mount up and make some tracks before they discover they're on a wild goose chase," he said, giving Consuela a hand up into the saddle, then lifting Benito and setting him in front of his mother.

They made a half-dozen miles before they had to take to the woods again to avoid more riders. In groups of twos and threes the Colonel's men were now spread out and scouring the countryside. Progress was slow. They played cat and mouse for the rest of the night, as several times searching riders passed within hollering distance.

The first blush of dawn's light found them still two or three miles from the mouth of the canyon.

"We've run out of dark," Shiloh said, reining close to Consuela's pinto as they picked their way through the heavy timber. "If they catch us in these woods come day, we're done for. We've got to make a run for it. Follow me and stay as close as you can. Can you make it?"

"We will make it," she said, nodding her head in confirmation.

Digging his heels in the big buckskin's flanks, they burst from the woods and headed for the riverbank. The pinto hung close. Coming to the water, they plowed across and climbed the bank on the far side. There were few trees or bushes on that side of the river and they made better progress.

Darkness gave way to light and light slipped quickly over the mountain and across the river valley. They rode hard, leaning forward in their saddles, urging their mounts to greater effort. The Colonel's hacienda came into sight on the mountain side of the river.

They sped past the fort-like enclosure within easy rifle range. It was just coming good day. Shiloh's hopes rose that they had not been seen, then felt a sick feeling in his stomach when a shot rang out, then another. Swinging a look over his shoulder, he saw four riders pounding out of the compound gate with their rifles in their hands.

Bending low, he snaked his Henry repeater from its saddle boot and replaced it with the pistolero's long barreled shotgun he had taken from the cabin. With the nose of the rifle, he swung an arch motioning Consuela to take the lead. She pulled up beside him.

"Up ahead the river runs through the mountain," Shiloh shouted across the narrow space between them. "Ride into it and wait for me there."

Twisting in the saddle, he snapped a quick look. The riders were rapidly closing the distance between them. Hauling back on

Buck's reins and stepping from the saddle in the midst of a skidding stop, he jacked a shell into his rifle and dropped to one knee. A puff of smoke rose from a distant rifle and Shiloh heard a swish as a bullet bit into the sand at his feet.

The riders spurred recklessly over the ground at full speed, bringing their rifles to shoulders. Shiloh steadied his shaking hands and laid his sights on the hard-charging sorrel in the lead and lifted the nose of his rifle slightly, allowing for distance. He drew in a deep breath and let it out in a slow slide and squeezed the trigger.

The Henry bucked against his shoulder. As if from an unseen hand the pistolero was swept from his saddle and tumbled end over end across the sand. The riderless horse swerved as its burden left its back.

Levering another round into his rifle, he found the chest of a second rider and triggered a shot that tore the man from his mount. His rifle flew from his grasp, hands clawing empty air.

The two remaining riders sawed reins and turned their mounts, quickly heading back the way they came. Readying his rifle again, Shiloh eyed the broad back of a retreating horseman and took careful aim. He touched the trigger and knew satisfaction when he saw the man's rifle slip from a hand and claw at his back. The rider reeled in his saddle and doubled forward as his horse charged onward.

Off in the distance, a cloud of dust told Shiloh he hadn't bought them much time. Remounting, he hurried to catch up with Consuela and the boy. She waited just inside the opening, her pinto standing uneasily in belly-deep water.

Reaching a gloved hand, he grasped the reins of her mount and led it behind his own horse as they moved at a slow walk down the rushing river. Solid rock walls on both sides formed a narrow tunnel and reached into the sky. The roar of the waterfall up ahead was deafening. They moved deeper into the canyon.

Swinging an anxious look over his shoulder he could see no one following but his quick gaze revealed fright on the faces of his companions.

"Don't worry," he assured them. "It'll be all right."

Coming to the cutback split in the rock wall he had discovered earlier, he urged the big buckskin out of the water and into the tight passageway. Stepping down, he transferred the boy into his own saddle and helped Consuela from the pinto onto the floor of the opening.

"Take the buckskin's reins and climb ahead of him," Shiloh told her hurriedly. "No matter what, don't stop. It's steep, but you can make it."

Without questioning, she took Buck's reins and started climbing. She's quite a woman, Shiloh mused, allowing himself a moment to stare after her.

Shaking the pleasurable thought from his mind, he hauled on the reins of the reluctant pinto.

Consuela and the buckskin were out of sight before he was able to convince the pinto out of the water and into the narrow opening. For a long moment the frightened animal stood, shaking nervously. Reaching a hand, Shiloh patted the horse on the neck.

"You'll be all right big fellow," he said in a raspy whisper. "If the buckskin can do it you can too."

They started the climb.

The pinto was considerably smaller and lighter than the buckskin and, once he got started, climbed gamely. He took the steep incline in short leaps.

Shiloh felt slack in the reins and struggled to stay ahead of the lunging horse. His wounded arm tugged on the reins, while his other used the butt of the rifle to pull himself forward. His lungs pleaded for air. His leg muscles knotted. Still he climbed on.

He wheezed down a ragged draught of air, sucked it up in great gulps. The pinto panted hard, breathing heavily and expelling a snorting sound from its nostrils with each leap. Up ahead, the buckskin was still nowhere to be seen.

After an eternity measured only in minutes, they broke out on top. Shiloh's buckskin stood quavering, sweating profusely. His head hung low. White foamy lather covered the big gelding's neck and withers and dripped from his belly onto the ground.

Consuela sat on the flat, rocky surface holding the buckskins reins. Benito sat beside her. One look told Shiloh she was completely exhausted.

"We'll rest here a few minutes," he said, dropping the pinto's reins. "You done well."

She offered only a weak smile.

Staggering across the solid rock surface, he peered over the edge of the cliff at the river far below. A scattering of horsemen milled about in the water, searching, seemingly confused by the disappearance of their quarry. Colonel Mattox sat his horse at the entrance of the canyon, shouting threats and orders.

The Colonel's head hinged upward, his gaze crawled up the sheer walls of the canyon and trailed along the rim toward where Shiloh lay, his head protruding over the edge. He quickly drew his head back. They would find him, he knew without a doubt, but he would make them pay dearly for the privilege.

He waited a few minutes and chanced another look. The riders had spread out, walking their horses slowly down the swift stream. One big pistolero was more reckless than the others. He had walked his bay farther downstream than the rest—too far. As Shiloh watched, the swift water caught his bay and swept them both downstream toward the roaring falls.

The horse fought frantically but foundered in the boil of the current, helpless against its strength. It was too swift, too strong. Abandoning his mount, the big pistolero tried swimming on his own but despite all his efforts he could not compete with the current and was carried toward the falls. His terrified scream was barely audible above the deafening roar of the water as both he and his horse were swept over the edge.

Seeing their compadres fate, the other riders turned their horses back towards the mouth of the canyon. Maybe they were giving up. Maybe they wouldn't spot the crack in the rock wall.

Suddenly a shout went up. What Shiloh feared would happen, happened. One of them had spotted the cutback opening.

Pushing to his feet, Shiloh strode back to Consuela's side.

"We've got to move higher," he told her, reaching a hand to help her up. "They've found the opening. They'll be coming soon."

The look on her face hurt his heart. It was a look of desperation, of resignation, of defeat.

"Don't give up," he tried to reassure her. "We're not beat just yet. Let's move you and Benito up yonder behind those rocks. You'll be safe there. They won't get up the passageway, I'll see to that."

Lifting the boy into the saddle, then giving Consuela a hand up, he swung onto the buckskin and set out toward the rock field. He figured it would take the Colonel's men maybe fifteen minutes to climb the steep trail.

If they did, he'd be waiting for them.

Hurrying along the now familiar trail, they wound their way through the rock slide and reached the edge of the scrub cedar thicket.

"Follow that trail," he said, aiming an arm at the barely visible break in the seemingly solid wall of the thicket. "When you come out you'll see an opening between two big rocks. Go through there and you'll find a little clearing on the other side. Wait there for me."

He didn't wait for an answer, there was no need of one. Like he had done his whole life, now he would do what needed doing. He wheeled the buckskin and started back down the way they had come.

Arriving near the outlet of the crevice opening, he ground-hitched his mount and fed the Henry rifle until it had a full load of fifteen .44-4 cartridges. Withdrawing the long-barrel shotgun from the saddle boot, he snapped it open and fingered in two double-ought shells before clicking it shut with a flick of his wrist. He raked back both hammers..

Crouching to one side of the opening, he waited...and considered what he was about to do. Once again it had fallen upon him to kill. To send others to join the growing line of marching dead that returned nightly to interrupt his sleep with haunting nightmares. Why? Why must he always be the one to right every wrong?

Then his thoughts flicked back to the sight he had witnessed at the village. In his mind the picture flashed clearly. The memory of men, women, older folks, children, all innocent victims of an evil man's hatred. All with necks crooked grotesquely, hanging from the bell tower of the mission. Shiloh's brow creased. His jaw set. His pale green eyes took on a familiar hardness.

He heard them coming.

They were on foot. Their steady stream of curses were recognizable in any language. When Shiloh figured they were getting near to the top he raised the shotgun waist high, pulled back both hammers, and stepped out.

His quick glance revealed at least a half-dozen pistoleros, maybe more. They climbed all bent over, near crawling on hands and knees, struggling up the steep incline. He touched one of the triggers.

The full load of double-ought buckshot hit the men like a swarm of angry hornets, tearing at the ones in front, ripping great chunks from their faces and chests. Showers of blood splayed down the narrow corridor, splashing the gray rock walls with a splattering of red. Screams of agony rose above the roar of the waterfall and filled the morning air.

Those farther back in the line that were only wounded by the first blast turned to flee, only to be overtaken by yet another burst of deadly pellets. Death hung like a thick cloud in the narrow passageway.

Blue smoke from the twin blasts surrounded Shiloh and drifted upward as he dropped the shotgun and scooped the Henry rifle into his hands.

Again and again he fired. The booming blasts barely blended before another cartridge was levered and sent ricocheting down the narrow rock tunnel. In a dozen heartbeats he emptied the gun. In a dozen more he fed another fifteen brass cartridges into the hungry weapon.

Stepping to the edge of the rock precipice, he peered down.. A scattering of mounted pistoleros whipped their horses, urging a faster retreat from the river. Their mounts struggled to obey, but the deep water prevented anything faster than a hurried walk. Flicking a sweeping look, Shiloh felt disappointmen. The Colonel was nowhere in sight.

Shiloh's hands made sweat inside his gloves. He raised the rifle to his shoulder. Bypassing those nearest him, he set his sights on the one closest to the mouth of the canyon. Finding the center of the fleeing man's back, he adjusted for the fall of the show, and squeezed the trigger.

The Henry blasted. A finger of flame spewed from the barrel. A puff of black smoke rose.

Down in the river, a pistolero spun crazily from his saddle, rolling like a ball into the swift water. His frightened mount trailed loose reins in the water as it plunged the few remaining leaps that carried it out of the confines of the canyon.

Methodically, Shiloh repeated the deadly process. When it was over, twelve riderless horses milled about, frightened and seemingly uncertain why they were suddenly free of their usual burdens.

Looking downstream toward the falls, Shiloh saw the river cleansing itself as the last of the bodies were swept over the edge of the roaring mass of water, carried hurriedly toward an unknown watery grave. Turning away, he scooped up the long-barrel shotgun and walked toward his waiting buckskin.

CHAPTER XIII

He found Consuela and Benito sitting huddled together under the big pine tree. Their anxious eyes lifted and filled with relief as Shiloh rode through the opening in the rocks into the tiny, grass covered valley.

She rushed to his arms as he stepped from the saddle. Sobs shook her young body and happy tears wet his shirtfront. Benito's small arms encircled his legs in a tight hug. Shiloh closed his eyes and lost himself in the rapture of the moment, a moment that would occupy a permanent place in his scrapbook of memories.

"Is it over?" she finally asked anxiously.

"It won't be over until the Colonel is dead," he whispered hoarsely. "But they'll lick their wounds for awhile I reckon. We best get some rest and some food in our stomach. There's a small coffeepot and the makings in my saddlebag and I think there's a little food in there, too. I'll go see if I can jump up a rabbit or squirrel directly."

Consuela began to lay and light the fire while Shiloh slid the big Sharps buffalo gun from its backward saddle boot, took the brass field glass from his saddlebag and threaded the ammunition belt with an arm.

"Tell Benito not to be alarmed. I'm gonna lay a couple of shells down among 'em so they'll keep their heads down."

Consuela and Benito walked over to the little rock tank to fill the coffee pot as Shiloh bellied down on the edge of the rock bluff overlooking the Colonel's hacienda. Extending the telescoping glass, he brought it to eye and gazed down into the walled compound.

The place was a beehive of activity with people running here and there. Two pistoleros had gathered the dead men's horses and were leading them toward the jumble of adobe huts upstream. A Mexican with a rifle stood guard at each gate. Four saddled horses stood tied to the fence at the corral. One of them was the one Colonel Mattox had been riding.

Swinging the field glass upstream, Shiloh saw several wounded pistoleros being helped along by their compadres. They seemed headed toward the jumble of adobe huts where they obviously lived. They had taken a serious beating and Shiloh wondered to himself what their next move would be. One thing for sure, they weren't just gonna forget about him and leave him up on that mountain.

He had watched for half an hour or so before he saw the door open and three tough looking hombres that looked like Americans emerged. Those were undoubtedly the Colonel's three lieutenants the padre had told him were along when the villagers were hung. They seemed headed for their horses.

Thumbing a handful of shells from the ammunition belt, he opened the gate and fed them into the big Sharps buffalo gun and slammed it closed. Thumbing back the hammer, he brought the long rifle to shoulder and laid the end sight in the center of the lead man's chest. Capturing a long draught of air, he let it out slowly, held his breath, and squeezed the trigger.

The big rifle slammed into Shiloh's shoulder. Before the deafening boom sounded, the man below was lifted off his feet and hurtled backwards. The big slug drilled into his chest and blossomed out the back in a fine red spray. For a long instant his two companions were frozen into confused inaction. Then spinning on their heels, they disappeared into the house before Shiloh could get off another shot.

"That ought to keep their heads down for a spell," he breathed aloud.

Pushing to his feet, he smelled the coffee. A little cloud of steam puffed from the bubbling pot and trailed into the air. The sweet aroma joined with the scent of pine and fresh mountain air to form a pleasing invitation. He followed his nose.

Consuela had found what was left of the meager food supplies in his saddlebags and laid it out near the fire. A small pan of black Mexican beans were starting to boil. He'd go see if he could find them some kind of meat before night set in. Glancing up, he saw the sun sliding toward the top of the mountain.

"Stay here," he whispered. "I'll be back in a bit."

Trading the Sharps long gun for his Henry, he strode quickly through the opening and from their little hidden space. He headed into the thicket of scrub cedar, bending and pushing his way through, kicking at the clumps of bunch grass as he walked. He hadn't gone more than forty yards before jumping a big jackrabbit. Shouldering his rifle, he quickly bagged their supper.

He could smell the coffee way before he got back to their camp. Quickly skinning and dressing the jack he handed it to a smiling Consuela. She washed it, ran a spick through it, and hung it over the fire.

"That coffee shore smells good," he told her, squatting near the little fire and accepting with a smile the tin cup Benito handed him.

Consuela used the tail of her skirt to lift the blackened coffeepot and pour his cup brimming full. He blew the steam away and chanced a tentative sip. He felt the pleasant burn of the hot coffee against his lips. It was too hot to taste but just the smell pleased his empty stomach.

"It's mighty good," he told her.

"Gracias," she said.

While their supper cooked over the fire, they talked. Not of killing, or hurt, or hatred, but of small things such as the sound of the soft breeze whispering through the pines, the crimson glow of the sunset creeping over the western mountain peaks, the white clouds drifting lazily overhead, the beauty of the tiny clearing where they were.

He watched her face as she talked. It was a strong face, and yet a face that smiled easily, even in the midst of their trouble. It was a face that asked little for herself, yet demanded everything for those she loved.

"What do you want from your life?" he suddenly whispered, not sure he was ready for her answer. "What would bring you happiness?"

Her dark eyes lifted to his. For a long space of time her penetrating gaze probed deep into his very soul, searching, questioning, seeking an answer to her own unasked question.

"You," she finally whispered, daring to voice what her heart was screaming out.

It was one of those memorable moments that would last a lifetime. One of those times you wish would never end. And in those moments Shiloh knew without a doubt he loved her with all his heart.

"What do you want?" she asked. "What would make you happy?"

He swung a look toward the golden glow of sunset. A lump climbed into his dry throat. A flush warmed his heart. A tiny tear trickled down his cheek. If only...If only I could dare hope, he thought.

"Back home I've got a piece of land that's as pretty as anything you could ever imagine. When I get back I'm gonna build a house on it—a log house—low and rambling—a place of my own with lots of room to grow a family. A place on that sloping hillside, with a big front porch where I can sit with a hot cup of coffee on a frosty morning and see the mist rising over the valley, and watch my cattle grazing on the tall, green grass.

"But a place like that wouldn't mean much unless I had someone to share it with. Someone like you, the way I see it, being happy ain't in the getting, it's in the giving. If you'll have me, when this is over, I'll be asking you and Benito to come back home with me, to share my dream."

A soft hand reached out and took his. Tiny silver tears escaped her eyes. A small smile lifted the corners of her beautiful lips.

"We will go," she whispered softly. "We will go."

Their eyes sought and found each other. No more words were spoken, there was no need of any. For in those few moments the promises made by their eyes and hearts were somehow more meaningful, more lasting, than any words could ever convey.

She spooned a helping of black beans from the small pan sitting over the fire into the only tin plate, added a rabbit leg and two tortillas from the small stack, and handed it to him. Kneeling beside Benito, she folded her hands in her lap.

Lifting the plate near his face, he anxiously scraped a spoonful and headed it toward his mouth. He was starved. Over the spoon, he saw them both sitting there, waiting patiently for him to eat his fill before they shared what was left. Lowering the spoon, he handed the plate to Benito.

"I forgot myself," he whispered. "In my family, the youngest always eats first."

The surprised boy flicked an inquiring glance at his mother. His hungry eyes went back to the plateful of food, then again to his mother before she smiled knowingly and nodded. He split a big grin and reached out to take the plate.

"It is a nice thing you do," she said, offering an appreciative smile.

He felt good. Her look warmed his heart. He sipped his coffee and watched the hungry boy devour the food. When should he tell her about her father and aunt? How could he pile more bad news on her right now? He decided nothing would be served by telling her until *and if* they got through what they still faced.

After supper he prowled a circle around the little valley. Over to one side, hidden behind some low bushes, he found a small space between the rocks. It wasn't much, but big enough for Consuela and the boy to squeeze into. Leading them over, he showed them the opening.

"When they come, I want the two of you to hide in there and wait. No matter what, don't come out until I call you."

"Will they come tonight?" she wanted to know.

"I doubt it," he said. "I don't figure they'll want to tackle that river in the dark. They'll most likely wait until morning and try to find another way up the mountain."

"Is there another way?" she asked.

"I don't know. If there is, they'll find it."

"That fellow up there on that mountain ain't human!" Ben Jeffcoat complained. "He's done killed half our men and now he put a bullet right through Frank's chest. Blowed a hole big enough to run a ax handle through."

"It was just a lucky shot," Colonel Mattox tried to convince them. "There isn't a man alive that can hit anything from that far away, and shooting down at that."

"Might try telling that to ole Frank," the obviously shaken man said, sprawling into a chair. "He must be using a small cannon or something. I never seen anything like it."

"Come morning we'll settle it," their boss told them. "We'll slip out before light and find another way up that mountain. I'm going to personally throw him off of that cliff," the Colonel bragged.

"Boss, we may have a hard time getting those Mex to go back up there against that fellow. They saw what he done to their compadres awhile ago and they're scared to death." George Folsom said, finding the nerve to speak up for the first time.

"Tell them I'll shoot any man that refuses my orders," Mattox screamed, his face turning beet red. "You tell them!"

"Yes, sir," Folsom said meekly, dropping his gaze to stare at the red tiled floor.

"As soon as it gets dark, have someone get rid of Duncan's body. I don't want it upsetting señora Diego," Sam Mattox told them, "and get the men organized. I want every man that's able to walk spread along that mountain face by first light. Bring plenty of ropes. We'll find a way up that mountain and we'll deal with this fellow like we deal with everyone that gets in our way. Where is El Lobo and that dozen new men he promised me?"

"I don't know, boss," Ben Jeffcoat told him. "Nobody's seen hide nor hair of him since he rode out for Chihuahua a couple of days ago."

Without another word, the Colonel did a military about-face and marched from the room, his back stiff as a board, his head held high.

Incompetent fools! Sam Mattox thought, as he stormed out of the room. If only he had a few good men instead of these imbeciles. They're all cowards and morons just like the ones he had back there at the battle of the Hornets Nest during the war.

The cowards had turned tail and ran and he had gotten blamed for it!

They had court-martialed him! That bunch of idiots that posed as generals had actually court-martialed him!

That dirty Reb up there on the mountain—it was all his fault. He was the one that led that ragtag bunch of misfits in that bayonet charge. They had put his whole command to flight. Shiloh, they called him, he was like a cat with nine lives.

"Why must you always insist on being late for dinner?" Romana Diego reprimanded him sharply as Sam marched hurriedly into the dining room. "Juanitta can keep the food hot only so long, you know."

"I'm truly sorry, my dear," the Colonel apologized, lifting out a chair and at the far end of the long table. "There was some pressing business I had to deal with."

"What was all that dreadful shooting I heard?" she questioned. "Riders rushing in and out. I really wish you would put an end to all this disturbance. One cannot even think clearly with all that going on. It's disturbing"

"It will be taken care of tomorrow, my dear. Rest assured, it will be taken care of tomorrow."

Shiloh picketed their horses near the entrance to the tiny clearing. He knew his buckskin would warn him of any intruder. He picked up the sleeping boy and carried him to his own bedroll near the little hiding place he had showed them earlier. The pine needles would make a soft mattress for Benito and his mother.

"He's a fine boy," Shiloh whispered, staring down at the sleeping tot.

For several moments he and Consuela stood side by side in silence, watching the boy. She bent to brush dark hair from his face with the tip of a finger. He slept peacefully, lost in a world of innocence, and trust, and unawareness of the danger they all faced.

Shiloh glanced at the beautiful young lady standing beside him and stared long in deep meditation. *What if I fail them? What if I'm not strong enough, or brave enough, or wise enough? They will die.*

He was suddenly afraid in a way he had never known before, not for himself, but for them. A new weight of responsibility hung over him in a way he had never experienced: grave, constricting, overwhelming.

This woman and this small boy had become the world to him. Their welfare rested solely upon him. He could not fail them. He would have sold his soul to spare them what he feared was coming.

A soft hand touched his. Their eyes met. She came to him, with moonlight dancing in her eyes. She surged into his arms and he welcomed her. He gathered her up in the breadth of his hands and wrapped her into himself. He wanted her—needed her more than breath—more than life. He loved her to the very depth of his soul.

He lifted one hand to her cheek, feathered his knuckles along her jaw, and raised her face to his. Their lips met. Her kiss was sweet, and soft, and tender, and filled with undreamed of promises.

He didn't know what tomorrow might bring. He would deal with tomorrow when it came. All they had was now. They had tonight, and if fate smiled on them, they had the hope of many tomorrows.

Consuela had long since returned to lie beside her restless son.

Shiloh tossed and turned on the soft bed of pine needles under the giant pine tree. For a long time sleep eluded him. Finally, his weary body dragged by sheer exhaustion, he sank into an unsettled dream world. But with a form of sleep came the inevitable nightmares.

They came out of the hazy darkness of a moonless sky. The walking dead. Materializing out of nothingness into vague forms that took shape gradually in his tortured mind.

Their worn and tattered Confederate uniforms hung loosely over skeletal frames. They floated into single file and encircled their sleeping executioner in an ever tightening enclosure.

Sightless, condemning, accusing eyes probed deep into the conscious of his soul. I couldn't help it! His mind screamed out for audience. I didn't want to kill you. The colonel forced us to fight. It was kill or be killed. Still they continued to march around him, the circle ever tightening.

A clammy dampness of sweat and fear settled over him. The ghostlike forms lifted empty hands toward him as if pleading for something, but for what? Tremulous groaning from his own chest woke him.

His quickened raspy breathing rattled in the early morning stillness. His clothes clung to his body. His lungs wrung dry. Sleeving sweat from his brow, he was momentarily disoriented. He flung a quick, searching glance at his surroundings before remembering where he was.

Settling a gaze on the sleeping forms huddled under a blanket a short distance away, he smiled. Last night's memory sent a wave of delight spinning through him. For an hour or more he lay awake, his thoughts swirling. His enemy would come today.

Like a young mother delivering her firstborn, the eastern horizon labored in a hard-fought struggle before giving birth to the emerging dawn. Shiloh's ears strained, half expecting to hear screams of the earth's birth pangs. But the mountain silence was broken only by the happy chirping of birds and the wind swaying the top of the pine trees in a rushing rhythm that felt like blood coursing through his veins.

Pushing to his feet, he raked aside the gray ashes of last night's fire and coaxed the live coals into a blaze with some small twigs. He added larger sticks, and hung the leftover coffee over the hungry flames.

Stepping lightly so as not to wake the sleeping figures, he moved to the little pool of water and washed. The cool water felt good.

Consuela moved under the blanket. Her dark eyes flicked open and found him. A smile creased her lips. Her arms lifted to the sky in a long, lingering stretch.

"Good morning," his whispered voice greeted.

"Si," she agreed, mumbling sleepily and slipping quietly from beside her son. "It is the best morning of my life."

It was a quick breakfast ate mostly in silence. They both knew, but were unwilling to acknowledge, their enemy would come today and perhaps they would die. But if that's what fate had decreed, death could not rob them of last night.

Dawns full light broke clear and cool and swallowed up the darkness.

The scent of fresh mountain air mingled with the sweet smell of pine cleansed his lungs. A faint pink glow painted the eastern sky as Shiloh bellied down at the bluff's edge. He raised the field glass to an eye and swept the compound below with a searching gaze. He was puzzled that there was no movement. The Colonel's hacienda seemed deserted. Had they fled? Had they just pulled out during the night?

Swinging his glass up the valley and back along the mountain's face, he discovered the answer to his mind's wondering. A line of climbing figures were scaling the steep rocky cliff. Long ropes dangled to aid their ascent.

Hurrying to his saddle, he withdrew the Sharps long rifle and slung the ammunition belt over a shoulder. Quickly returning to his vantage point on the very edge of the rock bluff, he spread belly-down.

Experienced hands methodically opened the gate of the weapon, fingered a shell from the cartridge belt, fed it into the dark opening, and slammed the mechanism shut all in one continuous motion. Swinging the nose of the rifle along the mountain, it came to rest on a straggled line of climbing figures.

The first few climbers were already hidden from view by a bulge in the rock face. His sight settled on the next man in line.

It was a long shot, most likely close to a quarter of a mile. He blinked his eyes to clear his vision, drew in a deep breath and let it out in a slow slide of air.

The ear-shattering explosion of the big buffalo gun sounded like a cannon. The recoil slammed against his shoulder with the strength of a kicking mule. A cloud of bluish black smoke puffed and lifted upward. Even as the deafening sound thundered along the mountainside a small figure was snatched from the rock face and spiraled downward, his arms windmilling in the air.

Before the sound died Shiloh had loaded another cartridge and was searching for a target. He found it at the very tail of the line. Again the gun blasted, again a figure danced into space, hurtling to the rocks below.

For long minutes he waited, his field glass exploring every crevice, searching the rock face, seeking a target and finding none. He knew some of the climbers would have reached the top. They would be seeking him out in minutes.

Rising, he hurried to where Consuela and her son stood near the rock tank, hugging each other, upset by the shooting.

"It's time to go to your hiding place," he told her, meeting her searching gaze. "Here, take this sawed off double-barrel. It's already loaded. Wait until they come close, draw back the hammers, point, and pull the trigger. Don't come out until I call you."

She guided the boy under the low bushes and into the small opening. Turning back, she raised a hand and splayed her soft fingers along his cheek. Her eyes locked with his and held.

Shiloh slowly lowered his head. He saw her beautiful lips part in anticipation as he closed the distance between them, and felt the sweet, heated mingling of their breath. He took possession of her mouth, claiming and savoring, desirous and tender. The kiss merged their souls as surely as their lovemaking the night before had merged their bodies.

He didn't want it to end but he knew it must. He wanted it to go on forever but knew this moment may well be the only forever they would ever have. Reluctantly, he raised his head to stare at her one last time. A soft hand lifted and a curled finger traced along the wetness of his lips.

"I love you, Shiloh," she whispered, her voice quivering, eyes blinking away happy tears.

"I love you," his grating voice managed in a shaky breath. "You and Benito have brought meaning back into my life that I'd lost. I don't know what miracle made you love me, Consuela, but I swear, as long as I live, I will do my best to make you and Benito happy."

He stole one more moment to drink her in. The rising sun lit her face with a heavenly brightness. Glow from a thousand candle flames crowned her head and sparkled in her dark eyes, eyes giving birth to silver tears. He slammed his eyes shut to capture this final picture. He would carry that image of her with him into whatever world came after this. Wheeling, he trotted toward the saddles where his weapons waited. He didn't look back.

Snatching up the belt full of double-ought shells, he threaded it with an arm and shrugged it over a shoulder. Taking up the long barreled shotgun, he broke it open and thumbed in two fresh loads and leaned the weapon against one of the rocks that formed the entrance to their little hideaway.

Loading the Sharps buffalo gun, he eared back the hammer and leaned it against the big pine tree. He figured that would be his final fallback position.

Sweeping up his Henry rifle and a cartridge belt full of .44 shells, he slipped it over his other shoulder cross-crossing the bandoleers across his chest on top of his tattered serape. Feeding the Henry a full load of fifteen shells, he jacked one into the chamber.

Checking both of his twin Colt pistols to make sure they were fully loaded, he led their two horses over near the little water rock tank and picketed them in place. Pausing, he allowed his gaze to draw a circle around the place he would make his final stand. Deciding he was as ready as he would ever be, he turned on his heels and trotted out through the opening to face his enemy.

Selecting a partially buried, boulder maybe a dozen feet from the entrance to their hideaway, he hunkered down behind it and waited.

He felt the familiar tingling that began in the base of his spine and climbed up to settle on the back of his neck; he always felt it before a battle.

His energy was blazing hot. His mind was focused and controlled and compelling. He had a job to do. He would do what he had to do.

From where he lay, he had a clear view of the trail where it emerged from the cedar thicket. He knew that was their only means of approach.

He didn't have to wait long. The snap of a dry twig announced their arrival. He raised his rifle and sighted along the barrel.

One of the Americans he had seen earlier down in the hacienda led the way. He crept along the trail cautiously, his rifle held with both hands in front of him, his head swiveling nervously from side to side.

Shiloh sucked his lungs full of air and let it out slowly. He blinked his eyes to clear his vision. Muscles knotted. His heart pounded like the hooves of a galloping horse. He wiped his sweaty hands on his pants leg. Still he waited.

The American paused as he reached the edge of the thicket. His slow gaze explored every inch of the rocky hillside where Shiloh lay watching. After several minutes the man seemed satisfied and stepped from the shadows of the trail into the open.

Shiloh squeezed the trigger. The .44 caliber slug punched a hole through the man's breastbone. He rose to his tiptoes and staggered backwards, the rifle slipping from his clutching hands.

A movement off to the right caught Shiloh's eye. A pistolero had crawled into position under a low hanging cedar. A finger of bright flame spat from the end of his rifle. A bullet ricocheted off the boulder only inches from Shiloh's head, stinging his face with rock slivers.

Blinking away the rock dust, he sighted along the barrel of his Henry and touched the trigger. A shrill scream rewarded his effort. The pistolero slumped motionless.

Two rifles boomed off to the left, another far to his right. Slugs slammed into his boulder and whined off into space. Shiloh jerked up a few inches and triggered three quick shots in the direction of the rising puffs of smoke, knowing they were wasted shots. They were moving their men into position to pin him down. He knew he had to move while he still could.

Fingering shells from the belt across his chest, he reloaded the Henry and crawfished backwards on his belly towards the opening in the rocks leading to the sheltered clearing. Pushing to his knees, he propelled himself into a rolling ball and scrambled into the opening just as several slugs plowed furrows in the dirt he had just vacated.

A chance glance upward showed him a Mexican standing on top of the rocks overlooking their little clearing. His rifle was already leveled. Shiloh ducked back into the opening as a bullet bit deep into the rock. He levered his own rifle and brought it to shoulder, snapping off two quick shots.

Shiloh's shots tore into the man. A loud grunt sounded. The Mexican grabbed his stomach with both hands. His rifle rattled against the rocks. The man pitched forward, his body did a somersault in the air and landed near Shiloh's horses with a thud, causing them both to shy and tug at their picket ropes.

Scanning the other rocks high above him, he caught movement. Scooping up the long-barrel shotgun leaning against the rock with his free hand, he sprinted for the pine tree where his Sharps leaned against the giant trunk. Exchanging the rifle and shotgun for the big buffalo gun, he raised it to his shoulder and crawled the front sight along the nooks and crannies of the mountainside.

The top half of a man's head rose above a rock. Shiloh centered his target and feathered the trigger. The distant head exploded like a watermelon, sending blood and bone fragments flying in a splay.

A man appeared from behind a tree and sprinted for

the cover of another. He didn't make it. The big slug from Shiloh's Sharps overtook him in mid stride sending him tumbling down the steep incline.

Black smoke pinpointed another's location even as a bullet buried deep into the trunk of Shiloh's pine tree with loud thug. He laid the sight on the man's location and waited. It was a long minute before a man's frame rose above a boulder, showing from his shoulders up. Shiloh fired. Another man died.

For a long space of time all was quiet. He used the lull to reload all his weapons to full capacity. By his reckoning, he had killed six, plus another two while they were climbing the mountain, another in the compound. He had counted twelve riderless horses in addition to the unlucky one that had gone over the falls. That was thirteen more. All told, that came to twenty-two. How many more he faced, God only knew. So far he had been lucky.

When they came, they came in a rush, two abreast and firing as they poured through the opening. Shiloh let fly with both barrels of the shotgun then dropped it at his feet, snatching up the Henry. Bullets tore chunks from the thick trunk of the pine tree in front of him. He saw men falling and dismissed them, focusing instead on those still on their feet and running both to his right and left, shooting as they ran.

He fired the rifle from hip-high, his left hand grasped the barrel and swung the Henry's nose to capture a moving target, triggered a shot, levered a new load while he found yet another target and fired again.

A sharp pain tore into his left leg just above his knee. The burning flush radiated upward through his whole being. He knew he had been hit. He gritted his teeth against the excruciating pain and kept firing.

The rifle clicked on empty. Casting it aside, he filled sweaty hands with his twin pistols. Using the tree both for protection and to hold him upright, he hugged it, a pistol in each hand on either side of the tree, belching fire and red-hot nuggets of death.

Shiloh's right pistol clicked on an empty cartridge. Flinging it aside he clawed a handful of tree trunk and hung on. Suddenly he realized the shooting had stopped. Only the screams and curses of wounded and dying men rent the air.

Sweeping a quick glance around the death littered battlefield, his gaze saw no one still standing, save one. Colonel Samuel Mattox advanced in measured steps toward Shiloh's tree, his pistol leveled.

"Drop it or die where you stand!" Shiloh's raspy voice commanded.

The Colonel stopped dead in his tracks, not twenty feet away. His face twisted and distorted with pure hatred. Eyes blazed. His whole body shook uncontrollably. He hesitated for a long minute, his shaking hand still clutched the pistol.

"I won't say it again," Shiloh gritted out, each word spoken emphatically.

A few more seconds clicked by. The pistol finally curled from the man's fingers and dropped at his feet.

"I suppose you'll just shoot me now." Mattox said. It was a statement instead of a question. "Is that the way you southerners do it?"

Shiloh leaned against the tree for support and stooped to his saddle lying against the tree trunk. He loosed the leather pouch tied behind it and fingered the rawhide thongs loose. The pouch unrolled of its on accord. Six bayonets gleamed in the noon sun.

"If I had wanted to shoot you I could have done it before now," Shiloh said, selecting one of the evil looking weapons and pitching it in the dirt at the Colonel's feet. "No, Colonel, you've got to die the same way seven of my fellow prisoners died. These were their bayonets. I'm going to kill you with one of them. Pick it up!"

A look of disbelief washed across the former officer's ugly face.

His eyes dropped to the bayonet at his feet, then back to Shiloh's face, then down to his wounded leg. A thin smile curled one corner of his lips as he reached down and palmed the long bayonet.

Shiloh shifted his weight to test his wounded leg. A sharp pain jolted him. He staggered, then righted himself. *I've got to do this!* His mind told his body. *I'll never be free until this is over and done with.*

He gritted his teeth and set his jaw. His cheek muscles corded in sheer determination. He willed his mind to ignore the pain and stepped away from the tree.

Taking slow, deliberate steps, mostly dragging his left leg, he moved toward his enemy. The Colonel matched backward steps for each of Shiloh's forward ones. When Mattox was well away from where he had dropped his pistol, Shiloh tossed his own pistol aside and lifted his hand to the large neckerchief around his throat. He fingered it loose and pulled it from him revealing the rope scar that ringed his neck.

"You can't even hang a man right unless they're women or little children. I'm gonna cut you up like a hog before I kill you, Colonel. You're gonna die real slow and real hard just like those folks you hanged in the village."

Drawing his own bayonet from his belt scabbard, he bent his right knee slightly and moved it forward. His left boot make drag marks in the dirt as it followed.

The Colonel's smile had vanished. His eyes were now wide and filled with fear. Sweat appeared on his forehead and scored trails through the dust and dirt that clung thick on his face. He licked his dry lips.

Both men held their bayonets low and out in front of their bodies, the gleaming silver blades flat with the razor-sharp cutting edge turned inward. They shuffled in an awkward circle over the uneven ground, arms extended, shoulders hunched. Each delayed the moment of contact, waited for the other to make a move, to challenge, to reveal a weakness.

Testing the Colonel's ability, Shiloh lunged, trying a shallow jab, pulling it back at the last instant. Mattox swiped his weapon sideways, a move that would have laid Shiloh's arm open to the bone had he followed through. *He's no slouch,* he thought. *He's fought with a knife before.*

Quickly stepping inside, Shiloh pressed hard, clearing the way with two double slashes and a deep jab. Mattox retreated. Shiloh pressed him, keeping the pressure on with a faked jab and a triple slash.

Mattox sidestepped and tried a thrust. Shiloh's left hand shot out and clamped on the Colonel's wrist that held his bayonet. Shiloh twisted with all his might but couldn't dislodge the weapon. Meanwhile, Mattox's own free hand had found Shiloh's wrist. They wrestled with each other, each struggling to gain the advantage. Locked in a dance of death.

Their faces were only inches apart. Straining, muscles bulging, faces contorted. Shiloh could smell the Colonel's foul breath. On an impulse, he spat directly in the evil face. The distraction caused Mattox to relax his grip on Shiloh's knife hand. He shoved his opponent backwards, arching a wide slashing swing as he did.

Shiloh's bayonet knifed through the Colonel's shirt, laying open a shallow slice in the man's stomach from hip to hip. Blood sprung from the wound and painted his shirt and pants front crimson.

"That's just the start of it," Shiloh said harshly, sucking great gulps of air between every word.

He paused briefly to catch his breath. His eyes burned. His heartbeat thundered, pounding against the wall of his heaving chest.

He advanced on the terrified Colonel. Deliberately taking his time. Mattox backed off, his fear filled eyes searching frantically for a way out.

Flicking a glance over his shoulder, his eyes went wide in his chalky face, blank with horror. He had backed to the very edge of the cliff. He could retreat no further.

An eerie presence suddenly filled the air. A foggy cloud drifted out of the bright sunlight and shrouded the entire clearing in a thick grayness. Shiloh blinked his eyes to clear his vision. When he opened his eyes he saw them.

They came as they always did, the walking dead. They floated from the cloud and took their place in the familiar single file formation. But this time was different from all the others. Instead of circling Shiloh, as they always had before, they formed a half circle facing Sam Mattox. Their pleading hands lifted as they slowly advanced toward the terrified and shaking man.

Whether Mattox did it by accident or on purpose, Shiloh watched helplessly as the Colonel took another step backwards, his booted foot finding only thin air.

An ear splitting scream followed the falling man all the way to the rocky valley below. Suddenly the scream stopped.

The line of Confederate dead slowly turned to face Shiloh. The outstretched hands now hung at their sides. Shiloh couldn't be sure, but the faintest hint of a smile showed on their faces. The blank, sightless eyes that had haunted him for so many nights, now stared understandingly, and closed as if in a restful, eternal sleep.

In the blink of an eye they were gone. Somehow, Shiloh knew within himself his nightmares were over. The walking dead would never return. They had been avenged.

EPILOGUE

Shiloh stood quietly next to the old blind padre on the little hill behind the mission. Simple peeled wood crosses stood at the head of twenty-four fresh graves laid out in uneven rows. Consuela knelt on her knees between two of them. Benito stood beside her, clinging tightly to his mother.

They had been halfway to the village before Shiloh had found the courage to tell her about her father and aunt. She had taken it awfully hard and had ridden in silence the rest of the way.

"Something has changed you, my son," the old padre said. "The hatred that once filled your voice is no longer there."

"I'm ready to put it all behind me and get on with my life," Shiloh said softly, still staring at Consuela and her son. "There has been so much killing. So many have died by my own hand."

"I once told you that we are all instruments in God's hands. Those evil ones will now know the eternal wrath of God for their deeds. Perhaps you too were simply an instrument God used to bring that to pass. I perceive that you will now find the peace you have been searching for, my son."

"What will happen to El Aqua Dios?" Shiloh asked.

"It will go on," the holy man said. "Like life, some pass on, others come to take their places. Man will always thirst for God. What will you do, my son? What of Consuela and Benito?"

"We will be married," Shiloh whispered. "We will be a family."

"That is good, my son. That is very good."

~THE END~

About the Author

I was born and raised in eastern Oklahoma—formerly known as the Indian Territory. My home was only a half-day's ride by horseback from old historic Fort Smith, Arkansas, home of Judge Isaac C. Parker, who became famous as "The Hanging Judge."

As a young boy I rode the same trails once ridden by the likes of the James, Younger, and Dalton gangs. The infamous "Bandit Queen", Belle Starr's home and grave were only thirty miles from my own home. I grew up listening to stories of lawmen and outlaws.

For as long as I can remember I love to read, and the more I read the more I wanted to write. Hundreds of poems, songs, and short stories only partially satisfied my love of writing. Dozens of stories of the "old west" gathered dust on the shelves of my mind. When I retired I began to take down those stories, dust them off, and do what I had dreamed of doing ever since I was a small boy—writing historical western novels.